I0748264

Unsent Letters

A Fictionalised Memoir

Heather Smith

Copyright © Heather Smith, 2025
Published: 2025 by The Book Reality Experience
An imprint of Leschenault Press
Leschenault, Western Australia

ISBN: 978-1-923454-01-9 – Paperback
ISBN: 978-1-923454-02-6 – eBook

The right of Heather Smith to be identified as author of this work has been asserted by her in accordance with sections 77 and 78 of the copyright, designs and patents act 1988.

This book is a work of fiction and any resemblance to actual persons, living or dead, or locations, is purely coincidental.

All rights reserved. No part of this publication may be reproduced or transmitted in any form or by any means, electronic or mechanical, including photography, recording, or any information storage or retrieval system, without permission in writing from the publisher.

The book is sold subject to the condition that it shall not, by way of trade or otherwise, be lent, resold or otherwise circulated without the publisher's prior consent in any form of binding or cover other than that in which it is published and without a similar condition, including this condition, being imposed on the subsequent purchaser.

Cover Design by Brittany Wilson | Brittwilsonart.com
from an original concept by: Katharina Kühne.

Praise for Unsent Letters

A work of art, words skilfully woven to create a tapestry that depicts a life well lived, of love found and lost, of suffering and joy, and eventually the discovery of peace and wisdom.

Evocative of Mallorca, its people, of the changes that have taken place since the seventies, of the unchangeable: the mountains, especially the Serra de Tramuntana, the soil rich beneath one's feet, the trees and bushes. Above all the sea, our Mare Nostrum, our Mediterranean.

Last but not least, it is a song to love, friendship and family, to the land the author was born in, the land she chose to live in and the land she adores, where she would have been chosen to be born.

Samantha Meade-Newman Whittington
Procuradora de los Tribunales and writer.

I loved reading this book. Heather Smith has deftly woven together poignant observations of places, cultures and characters. At the end of each chapter, I looked forward to the next, wondering which location and character was coming because of the wonderful way the author captures and portrays detail. She also captures the essence of looking back over life experiences in a way that makes the book one of those special ones that stays with you after you have closed the cover.

Emma Ellis
Historian

For Steven and David

Before I Forget

Before I forget to look at the orange sun blinding me
As it spreads its liquid halo behind the hills at dusk,
Crepuscular, alien, astonishing, belittling,
Beyond beautiful, beyond understanding,
Before I forget to look at the cat slinking his way
Amongst the bushes,
                              the fledglings skimming low at dawn,
Before I walk away forever, I will remember this:

That this beauty, that this pain existed,
That this flimsy flesh, this broken loveliness
Was here on earth where I walked my time.
I will remember to look at the faces of friends,
Of my people, *mi gente.*
I will engrave the sweetness of one, the irony of another,
The anguished eyes of some,
                              the helpless gentleness of others,
The hidden disappointment of most.

And I'll take with me the diamond
                              of your generous hearts,
Which maybe I didn't deserve, but you gave me anyway.
Will it all fade, light as gossamer,
                              like the bougainvillea leaves

That fall paper-thin in dried crumbling exuberance,
Will none of this matter when I no longer remember,
Or will it live on as strands
                              threading through the universe,
Forever weaving and dancing in love and sorrow?

ONE

Palma

The idea of going away came to me when I was watching the news on the television. I had just returned from the doctor's and was slumped on the sofa in need of distraction. It was the twenty-fourth of October, the day they exhumed General Franco's remains from the majestic mausoleum at El Valle de Los Caídos, to transfer them to a more discreet resting place, forty-four years after he had died. I watched how his coffin was brought out to be aired for a few hours before being reinterred in a family tomb of lesser glory. It was wrapped in a wrinkled bronze cloth which rather resembled a gigantic shoe bag with drawstrings. It was the same one he had been buried in – according to the papers – and was borne by some of the male members of his family, black-coated and sombre-faced. And as they carefully manoeuvred the coffin down the steps that led to the waiting hearse, my mind wandered, and I began to imagine the youngest bearer at the head of the procession tripping and causing a kerfuffle as the others tried to steady the coffin. My irreverent mind pictured the Spanish flag that was draped across the bronze cloth slipping to the ground, and a sheen of sweat glistening on the self-righteous countenances of the coffin bearers in the hot Spanish sun. Order was regained, but none of the few flag holding onlookers would forget the sound of Franco's mummified body softly thudding against the padded confines of his eternal bed.

Imagination had always been my escape route when no physical one was possible and now there was no escaping the doctor's prognosis. But perhaps this time I could physically flee for a few months. Franco's disinterment had me thinking back to those first years when I would have given my right arm to be able to escape. I had been living on the island of Mallorca since 1970, when five years later, a tragic Arias Navarro, the dictator's last prime minister, announced Franco's death on television. Any signs of rejoicing were only expressed in private. That day in 1975 I had a dental appointment, and I sat in the chair imagining that the stony-faced dentist might drill a hole in my skull if he could have read my thoughts. In the last years before Franco's death, I had witnessed how Spain remained virtually isolated from cultural, political and social developments in Europe, despite timid efforts to change. Back then, I thought that when the steel clamp of dictatorship lifted and democracy finally seeped into the country's bloodstream, lo and behold, diehard mentality would undergo a magic transformation. Ideals and fantasies of a twenty-year-old. I wouldn't have to be apprehensive about being seen by my father-in-law or husband as I walked along streets that were not allotted for me to go down. For even then I liked to wander and feel the breeze, heavy with exhaust fumes, push through my hair. It was a thirty-minute snatch at freedom, more truly enjoyed than the mindless few years of liberty I'd had in England as a teenager.

I switched off my TV and plucked at the loose skin on my hands; the two arthritic fingers on my right hand were exactly like my mother's, I thought. I had lived almost fifty years on this beautiful Phoenician Island surrounded by the rotting Mediterranean, not that the tourists who swam in it seemed to care. Fifty years, from my youth to early old age. Franco's unearthed coffin with his corpse rattling inside was like a gigantic punch in the face. And I actually felt a quiver of sadness for him. I had lived through the last five of his forty years of pomp and glory. This is what we come to, with or without the glory.

I thought I must plan something unexpected, even outrageous, for this quite well-preserved nearly seventy-year-old who looked a bit like an ageing Shirley MacLaine, so people said; but not to give others a conversation topic for a couple of years before I was just another puff of smoke on the horizon. No. It was just for me. The effect of my plan on friends and relatives didn't bother me, because the unseen hand pushing me forward gave me no choice but to carry it out. I gave myself five months, until the end of March when my seventieth birthday would have been celebrated and done with.

Most people of my age would be content to sit on the sofa in the afternoons watching the soaps, with a weekly outing to the cinema and a family lunch on Sundays if their children still put up with them. Not me. Although of course I loved sitting in my old dressing gown, doing nothing but daydream or watching despicable pro-grammes which I could have despised myself for, but didn't. Would I soon end up eating toast for lunch in my pyjamas? There was a definite possibility. But these bouts of slovenliness were necessary to keep my dwindling energy resources up to a working level, or so I liked to kid myself. One thing that hadn't decreased with age was my vanity. I still dyed my hair, put on my make-up with the aid of a magnifying mirror and carefully chose my clothes. I wouldn't go out the house without matching underwear. Who was it for? Primarily for myself, but at the back of my mind there was the rapidly fading idea that I might still meet the right man. I hadn't yet accepted that life had cheated me in that respect; was still half-convinced that after thirty-four years of soul- and body-crippling marriage, I was due compensation. And what if the doctor's prognosis was inaccurate and I still had two or three years ahead of me, instead of a miserly twelve to eighteen months?

So, on that hot October day, with mosquitoes still feasting on my thin skin and all the signs of global warming undermining what could have been a luminous autumn day, a seed was planted in my overactive mind. And in part I had to thank Franco's disinterred coffin appearing from the depths of his grandiose mausoleum on the shoulders of his descendants. You could say that his re-exposure to the harsh sunlight was a reopening of Pandora's box, especially my box. Or was it more like a final closure of that period of time in history, which had also affected my own personal one, and an opportunity to give everything in it, good and bad, a final airing before putting the lid down again and starting afresh? It was a chance to look at things in broad daylight, with no filters, to understand what had really happened. No more self-justification, no more self-pity, just the hard, priceless freedom that comes with trying to accept the truth. The truth of desiccated corpses dressed in military regalia, and the truth of my nearly fifty years on the island of Mallorca.

November was sultry and stormy. Torrents, narrow mountain brooks, clogged with debris, plastic and natural, overflowed and caused minor floods. Most people tut-tutted and spoke sagaciously about climate change and global warming yet continued to use their large cars instead of the bus service and still didn't recycle their abundant rubbish. What's the point, when it all ends up in the same place anyway? they asked with a show of clever scepticism. The fact that this island might be among the first to disappear under rising sea levels was pushed to the back of their pragmatic minds. Live the moment, be here and now; wasn't that the new challenge? But the climate was in a state of rebellion and the stirrings of my soul mirrored it.

During that month the suffocating embrace of claustrophobia held me as I rattled around inside the white walls of my apartment; as I went on strolls to my favourite little beach in search of ducks and seabirds, only to feel hemmed in by this small sea. The older I got, the more my mind screamed for expansion, the stiffer my body became, the greater my awareness that it wasn't me. I felt the workings of the body I inhabited, and I feared their failing, like the arrhythmia of my heart. Yet I was not this physical heart, nor my childhood nor teenage heart. Not even my fluctuating emotions were me. Just what was me?

December, like all Decembers, was lived on the tip of

the family iceberg. The forced comings together, the over expense and the overwork of Christmas had me on the verge of exhaustion and rebellion, apart from a few sweet moments with my grandchildren. For that was just it; the sweetness of Christmas, the innocent purity, had disappeared, at least for me, under a mountainous tip of refuse. Human refuse. Greed and hysteria. No stillness, no holy night, unless you could escape to a retreat in the hills – not that I wanted to become a recluse and spend the rest of my days in meditation. No. But to recover the ability to withdraw and savour some kind of sacredness at certain moments, this upholds you, this is the net that stops you falling into the abyss of insanity.

Was it that I had a twinge of nostalgia for the Christmases of my childhood in England in the fifties and sixties, when our lives were not buried under this heap of consumerism? They might have been a bit twee with all those paper chain decorations that covered the ceilings, but at least the tree smelt real under its load of tinsel and gaudy balls. It was cheap and tacky, the presents simple, but carol singers would turn up at the gate and for me the dark cold of December that rushed in when the door opened to them was a portal to mystery and magic. Can people not cope with that kind of defenceless innocence and purity nowadays, are even challenged by it, so a kind of sophisticated cynicism is worn as protective armour? At my age, I no longer needed armour. I needed to shed the stifling layers and let my quivering soul wander free.

But January, New Year, new decade, time for change. Big plans. Thinking back over the previous year and trying to pick out moments of significance, I soon realised that most of the days were glued together in a lump of monotony and that if I didn't have to leave the house, I would hang around in my pyjamas until at least twelve o'clock, slumped on my comfortable sofa reading books, grateful if I was feeling well. But my inner landscape was undergoing a slow upheaval and, as it was always with me, that slow change rumbling underneath would suddenly erupt into action.

So, I inspected my bank account. Not a lot, but enough to keep me going for a year. Was it worth selling my car, a twelve-year-old dented Citroën covered in scratches from living in the street? I wouldn't get much for it, but I couldn't ask anyone to keep it for me without letting the cat out of the bag. And talking of cats, I would have to confide in my upstairs neighbour, the woman who always looked after my cat when I went on holiday. I would tell her I was going away for longer this time. She would keep an eye on my apartment, and I would tell her to use my little side garden. We lived in what had been a large holiday chalet now converted into three apartments. It must have been paradise here back in the fifties when it was built, only two streets away from the beach. But now tall blocks hid the sea, and the noise of traffic muffled the sound of the waves breaking.

My seventy-square-metre apartment had been home for nearly thirteen years. I didn't need more, and the little garden with its one orange and one lemon tree gave me something pleasurable to look out onto every day. It had started as an attempt at a Japanese zen garden when I first moved in. I had filled it with white pebbles that encircled the trees and two hibiscus plants. I had planted four bougainvillea, purple, pink, orange and white, against the wall that separated me from the house on the other side. They had grown wildly, hugely, intermingling in a startling display of colour for six months of the year. Now most of the white stones were covered in rotting hubris, and weeds grew through the ever-widening spaces in the cloth beneath them. I needed a gardener to cut back the trailing bougainvillea and generally clean up what I no longer had the inclination to do. But I was cutting down on all my expenses, making excuses for not eating out with friends, saying I wasn't feeling well or had some other commitment. I would make it up to them before I left. I would invite them all to a seventieth birthday dinner. Not long to go.

In February I made a few excursions into the countryside. I wanted to fill my retina with the spectacle of the flowering almond trees and the shapes of the blue-black mountains of La Tramuntana with their halos of cloud at dusk. Because Mallorca, whether you liked it or not, did seep under your skin, year by year, drop by drop. And there was no point in resisting, I'd realised; you just had to release yourself into that stream, that underlying current which gradually eroded all attempts at criticism. You'd be swearing at the traffic and noise one moment to be then transported into a luminous paradise of colour and ancient stone walls only half an hour's drive away; or you'd walk into the old quarter of Palma and only hear the seabirds squawking above in the narrow strip of sky that covered those centuries-old streets. I thought I hated the island those first ten years of living in this pro-Franco stronghold of Spain. But I had transferred the anguish of my unhappy marriage and the suffocating customs of that time to this tough diamond of an island that had suffered so much invasion and bloodshed. For Mallorca still shines despite the hordes that have damaged it in the past and now.

So, I drove out and stopped the car in places where I could walk in the small fields and touch the flaky bark of the stunted almond trees. Could I recapture the first astonishment at beholding those winter flowers, white and pink, on the spindly, ancient branches? Well, no, I couldn't. I'd seen them too many times to be over-whelmed by their beauty, by fields and fields of blossom and the first flowering weeds, wild *margaritas* and *vinagrilla* that covered the coarse grass with bright yellow. Against a background of green grass, still lush from winter rains, and the fertile, ruddy earth, the wildflowers and white blossom displayed themselves in long stretches behind the stone walls. But even though the spectacle delighted me, I was no longer moved. And I wanted to be moved. I wanted to be surprised like a child, to gasp in astonish-ment. My whole psyche needed a cleansing, an emptying out of debris, an airing of secret compartments where clogged memories and festering misery clouded a clear vision of what was out there, now, in that pristine Mal-lorcan light.

March. That was it. No going back. I had even started singing to myself; I hadn't done that since I was a teen-ager. There wasn't that much to organise. The neighbour would adopt my cat. The car was sold for three thousand euros. Now I had to tell family and friends at my seven-tieth birthday party. I had sometimes said how much I would like to get away, but no one had taken me seriously. They were just the whimsical thoughts of an old woman who would never dare to go off by herself. I was nervous on the day, but underneath there was a deep calm, as if an unseen hand were gently pushing me forward.

I had invited them to a dinner at a nearby restaurant. They were all there: my two sons, Tom and Sam (both divorced), with their four children, my grandchildren; my sister, Caroline, who had come especially from England for my birthday and was spending the last few days of her holiday with some old friends; my ex-sister-in-law, Marisol; and my closest friends, Cliona, María del Mar, María Consuelo and Alberto. I knew I would hurt them all with that lack of confidence, the holding back from the people I loved the most, the ones who had shaped the course of these seventy years at some stage or other. They would understand with time that I could not have done it in any other way.

The birthday dinner was held in a small Italian restaurant tucked up a side street near my apartment. We sat at a long table of polished cherry wood which gleamed under the candles in their glass holders. I had asked for there to be no tablecloth, just woven straw mats that would not cover the beauty of the table. By ten o'clock everyone was full and happy with wine, mushroom risotto, pasta and birthday cake, and my youngest granddaughter had fallen asleep on her father's lap. It was time. I had to be quick, even at the risk of seeming heartless, while I still had the courage to say goodbye to those beloved faces. I beckoned to the waiter to serve champagne. I was feeling strangely detached – or perhaps it was a defence mechanism – as I rose from the table, glass in hand to toast them, my family and friends.

'This has been a special birthday. As you know, I've just entered a new decade; not an easy one to step into with its connotations of real old age, possible illness, possible death before I reach the next one. I'm not being morbid, just realistic. You know how close to my heart all of you are, so close to the bone it can get uncomfortable, even painful at times. So don't ever doubt my love for you. You've given me some beautiful gifts, but the most important ones have been your being a vital part of this long, twisting journey. But now I'm going to give myself a gift. Tomorrow I'm going away. I don't know how long for yet. Maybe a year, maybe less.'

My little speech was interrupted by gasps of 'What?' '*¿Qué dices?*' '¡Mamá!' Then silence, which was broken by one of my grandchildren.

'Will you bring us a present back, Nanny?'

'Of course, I will.' I continued: 'I'll be travelling to several places during the year. And you'll be getting emails and WhatsApps to tell you I'm okay. No need to worry. I did try to give you hints but you didn't get the message. I need to find out who I am at seventy and who I want to be.'

'But why haven't you said anything before? And what will you do for money?' asked Tom, attempting to cover the fear that always lurked beneath his cool exterior.

'What if you get ill? You're so tired lately,' said Sam. 'And what about the kids? Who's going to look after them on Mondays?'

'Good for you!' histrionic María del Mar clapped loudly and raised her glass.

'You hid that well,' Marisol said with a false smile and shifted in her seat.

'But you, by yourself … at your age?' said María Consuelo, her upper lip curling in a lady-like sneer.

'Bravo!' Alberto said. 'Can I come and see you?'

'I can and can't believe it,' Cliona said in her soft Dublin accent.

'Well, you could at least have told me.' Caroline's eyes were welling up. 'Where are you going?'

'You'll find out sooner or later. As I said, I'll be going to different places, but you will get old lady postcards from wherever I am. Please don't worry. Be happy for me. If I get fed up, I'll come back, but that isn't my intention.'

'But tomorrow? Are you all packed, then?' Tom asked.

'Yes, tomorrow. And thinking of that, I ought to be going home. I must say goodbye, my lovelies. The bill is paid. Drink up the champagne! I love you.'

I left the restaurant while they were still under the effects of alcohol and shock. I didn't look back, especially as I didn't want to see the hurt in my sister's eyes. I went home swiftly, locked the door and turned off my mobile. My two suitcases, bursting with clothes, pills and photos, were waiting by the front door. A taxi would be picking me up at five a.m. the next morning to take me to the airport.

Courage had failed me when I said goodbye. My diagnosis would remain a secret till my weakness could no longer be disguised.

TWO
Sidmouth Junction

Feniton, Devon

Friday 27 March

Dear Caroline,

Yours is the first letter I'm writing. Please don't be offended by my sudden departure. This is the only way I can find out who I can be, am, at seventy. I need to say goodbye to all the ghosts of myself who I hardly recognise, or just integrate them honestly, with all their nasties too. I know you'll come to understand why I needed to go on this journey. But please stop comparing yourself to me; don't judge me, at least not yet. We have different needs, different mechanisms for working things out, all equally valid. You are the fairy queen, unique and beautiful in the fragile world you have built for yourself. I think of you in your wild garden, feeding the squirrels and birds, marvelling at the flowering weeds that grow between the cracks of the paving stones. You have your little haven, a refuge from the roughness and rudeness of the outside world. It's a lonely one at times, I know, but you don't put up with intruders for long.

In the haze of my early years your face is the first one to appear in my life, after Mum and Dad's. I could have started my journey in Brighton, but I don't remember myself then, so I began in the West Country, that precious corner of England I loved so much, where we spent seven years of our childhood. We were the true railway children, picking primroses along the banks and getting free rides up front in the engines, watching how the driver shovelled in the coal. Do you remember? We were so close then, in that childhood innocence when we didn't judge each other but just let each other be. You were my protective big sister, and I was the little nuisance who interrupted your quiet games, but there was no envy or competition.

I'm staying in a B&B in Feniton. The village hasn't changed much, thank God, and nor has the smell of fresh earth, damp grass and rotting leaves, but I walked down to Railway Cottages at Sidmouth Junction, where we lived those three years, and found nothing. They have been erased, the little station demolished, and in its place there's a bus station for the use of the inhabitants of the horrendous housing estate that covers all those beautiful fields. I suppose I should have been prepared, because before coming here I drove to Milbourne Port station in Somerset (I've actually hired a car and have overcome my fear of driving on the left). Well, Dad's first station as stationmaster has been converted into a house! Yes, our station house from where we used to watch the old steam engines chug through has been taken over by some rich bastard. You can still see where the old lines were, but the platforms have gone. I felt quite empty and forlorn standing there, overwhelmed by how ephemerous and insubstantial our physical lives are. We can only recreate them in our memories, while we still have them. Is it all a fiction in the end?

I have to admit that even though it was to be expected, I'm deeply disappointed. I'm beginning to regret coming back. Our little childhood ghosts could have remained there safely, still wandering freely along the muddy lanes. Mine in particular would be roaming the softly swelling hills, surveying the land as if it was my own. My childhood paradise has vanished, and in its place, there stands a sacrilegious housing estate. The houses are all built of the same red brick, same size, same shape. So typical of England, they are uniform boxes with identical, oblong gardens separated by flimsy fences. Some of the gardens have immaculate lawns; others, just bare earth sprouting weeds. There's a lack of solidity about them, a lack of beauty, of character, of soul. A deficit of imagination. Or money? Maybe both.

I'm on the verge of tears as I remember those lush fields, the red earth and the buzzing hedgerows. The ghost of myself from two to nine years old is weak and fading with every day I spend here. I look at the black and white photos I've brought with me to remind myself that some part of me did live here in the 1950s. I want to remember you at that time, too, so I look at the ones of us together in front of the cottage in our Sunday best, large bows in our hair and sashes around our homemade dresses. Does any of this still live within me or you? Or were we two little egos running around in a heaven soon to disappear? But before I truly lay this phantom to rest,

I'd like to give it a little airing and observe it before the lid goes down.

Also, I want to observe you and try to imagine what it was like being my older sister. I was raw and unhindered back then, but you always seemed to be reserved and quiet, even at the age of nine or ten. I never knew what you were thinking. But now I think you were already dazed from what the world had thrown at you and were taking time to come round. What did you do when I was off on my long walks or cutting caterpillars in half to see what was inside? I often had a desire to bother you, just to see you react. Funny how then I was the little sod, annoying like a boil on the backside, and you became more rebellious in your middle years, when you decided how unfair life had been to you and you let all that suppressed anger out, especially on the ones you thought were to blame.

But maybe you were always watching me covertly, seeing what I was up to, loving and hating me, protecting me as we got older, even into the early years of my married life. Did it give you a feeling of superiority, as older sister? Maybe, but I feel it was also out of love and an almost masculine need to protect. When I became less vulnerable, your role had to change. You weren't used to being on an equal footing.

Of course, like all siblings we had our secrets and not-so-secret jealousies and rivalries, but it was not until we became adults that I realised how well you had concealed your jealousy of me. I thought I was the jealous one then, especially of your beauty. How I envied your blonde plaits, which I wasn't allowed to have because according to Mum, 'they didn't suit me'. And so, I was given a pudding-basin haircut which never grew beyond my ears. Mum wasn't even moved when I fabricated my own string plaits which I attached to another piece of string tied round my head. Do you remember? You used to laugh at them. Even then I had a need for beauty, or maybe it was just burgeoning vanity. Now when we sit together, I'm reminded of two old birds hunched up, preening what's left of their feathers.

We grew up tough down there, didn't we? No running water, one weekly scrub in the tin bath that hung on the outside wall next to the lavatory. Remember how Mum, resigned and resentful, had to fill it with water she carried in buckets from the well and then heated in cauldrons on the stove. Dad was the first to get in, we two the last, screaming if we saw a worm floating. Our frustrated, irritable mother, a townie who had been uprooted to the wilds of Devon, had no patience if we fell and cut our knees on the vicious stones that formed the pathway leading to the cottage. Money and her temper were short. She didn't like the hard grind of country life and often took it out on us, especially you. Your slowness irritated her, and she couldn't show you the patience and love you needed. It was Dad, so often absent from our lives, who understood you more. You were always falling over, losing your balance with your bad back and feet. Watching me who had none of those physical problems must have been hard to swallow for a kid. But I've stopped feeling guilty for being the 'more privileged' daughter. What could I have done about it anyway? When you wonder what you were doing here on earth, what your existence mattered, I can tell you that you gave the world your beauty.

I took a train ride to Ottery St Mary today. I wanted to see our old primary school. It's still there but so modernised you wouldn't recognise it. Yet I could still see us dressed up as pixies on Pixie Day and dancing round the maypole. I walked past the thick cobbled stone wall of St Mary's which led to the Catholic school where our neighbour Mary went. Her school always seemed more mysterious and magical than ours. Where were you when Mary and I made those altars with little statues of the Virgin Mary on the mantelpiece of my bedroom? Dad was deeply concerned I was under the influence of Catholicism at the age of seven! You were absent from all that, my first skirmish with another religion outside C of E which meant belonging to the village church choir and going to excruciatingly boring Sunday school. I wanted the sacred beauty of ritual, but Mum, who hated all religion anyway, thought of it as a passing phase. Remember how she used to call Dad a hypocrite if he went to church after kicking the cat! But I needed to drink from some source of spirituality from an early age. I think you were content to believe in the fairies that lurked behind every tree in the woodland. And you would have stayed with the fairies if you'd been given the chance, if we hadn't been dragged from these dells and hills into outer London suburbia.

Remember how we used to travel everywhere by ourselves, on foot or by train? There seemed to be no danger back then, did there? But one of my most vivid memories is of how at the age of nine I was touched up by a man on the train. You remember there were corridors in most trains then. I was seated by the window, alone in one of the carriages of a practically empty train that ran from Sidmouth Junction to Honiton. He came in and sat opposite me, a sandy-haired guy of about twenty-five. 'You've got nice knees,' he said, smiling. I smiled back in my nine-year-old innocence and in a flash, he was sitting next to me, one arm around my shoulder, hand up my skirt and then his fingers probing inside my knickers. When I started to cry, he got scared and bolted.

That first encounter with a man invading my defenceless body left a deep impression on me. I told no one, only you years later. Now when I think of him there is something that reminds me of Javier, something similar in the colouring and that uncontrolled sexual depravity, in the staring blue eyes, something darkly disgusting which I tried to shrug off in my teens. Perhaps if I had talked about it there and then, it wouldn't have festered, but we were never encouraged to express our emotions or traumas, were we? So, I carried it with me and became more silent.

Before I pack my bags again and move on, I want to tell you this: we are old women now, and old age does have its advantages. Because there is a return to simplicity, a shedding of a few layers of the ego which makes us more transparent to one another. The estrangement of our middle years, all down to our disagreement over Mum, has disappeared. I can see you as the awkward little girl and gangling teenager, the young woman who tried to protect me from Javier at all costs. I can reconnect with your fierce innocence before you became embittered from all your physical suffering and the feeling of not being loved. I can understand your anger, which is just your way of covering up fear and unexpressed sorrow. You are so strong and so vulnerable. But before we get to the point where our lucidity fails or an illness knocks us over, I want you to know how much I love you, how grateful I am for your protection in the bad times, and how sorry I am for my own pig-headedness when I refused to see or rather to feel your viewpoint. Mum's influence lay heavy on us both and in her last years created a wall between us. Time to knock it down and let the roses grow through.

When I'm back, let's go to that five-star hotel in Deià and spend a weekend surrounded by the bougainvillea, the jasmine bushes, and the mountains with their misty wreaths. My childhood paradise has relocated to my memory, but there are still a few corners left of the one in Mallorca. It's been a few years now since you smelt the pine resin in the heart of this island.

You always said it was your fault I ended up in Mallorca, that you came here for me so I could work out some twisted destiny. But now I wouldn't live anywhere else. We often talk about how I came to spend my summer holiday with you that fateful 1969. I remember your Thomas Cook's blue rep uniform; how different you were to when you languished in England. The Mediterranean lifestyle brought out the best in you and the hot climate suited your bones. But as for me, a nineteen-year-old student from Manchester University, my carefree existence was about to be shattered with the appearance of Javier in my life. Fate often needs an accomplice, and that was your role when you took me out that night. I can recreate the evening I met him perfectly. Let me tell it again, so I can finally bury it.

Remember how we walked into the open-air disco on that hot August night? It was called Babalú. I'd never seen a disco set up in a garden before, with tables and chairs spread out, as if we had been invited to an informal garden party. The sweet smell of night jasmine, *dama de noche,* pervaded all and predisposed us for romantic encounters, or just plain pick-ups. Now it's a shabby go-karting race-track!

We looked good then, didn't we, with our long, tanned legs and short skirts. I was wearing a red minidress and thick black eyeliner, my gamine haircut like a shiny helmet. You were wearing a more romantic, flared dress and your blonde hair floated about your shoulders in nurtured waves. Two naïve, pretty girls of nineteen and twenty-two. One was to be lured into the den of a local wolf; the other carried on with a reasonably normal life. I still wonder what my life would have been like if I hadn't met Javier that night. Useless wondering, I know.

I first noticed Javier when we sat down at a table. He was leaning against a whitewashed wall, hand on hip, sizing up the girls with feigned nonchalance. But I wouldn't have given him a second glance if he hadn't suddenly appeared at our table and asked me to dance. He didn't even look Spanish, with his light-brown hair and pinkish-white skin, although his broad nose and heavy features showed Moorish genes. He also danced with his hand on his hip in some kind of weird courting ritual. I thought he was ridiculous and not my type at all. I liked guys with a moderate hippy flavour, but he was too well dressed in his pressed light-blue trousers and immaculate white shirt. His hair looked coiffed and sprayed, and his unblinking blue eyes gave me the creeps. Needless to say, I refused a second dance and hurried back to the table. He looked nonplussed, as if no one had ever refused a dance with him before. But after a while he came to our table again and said, 'Can I talk to you for five minutes?' The die was cast by those eight words. Words that would overturn my naïve plans for the future and trap me for thirty-four years. He was a magician with a tongue that could spin more tales than *Don Quijote* and make you believe what he wanted. I soon forgot the clothes, his hair, his short stature and the pose. He made me laugh constantly, deep belly laughs, the tears rolling. He was powerful and hypnotic with a strange nervous energy, different to anyone I had known. You were taken in by him too. We both believed he was a French pilot. I did question his French, but he said it was a dialect. How pathetic we were!

That was Javier at his best. He was witty, imaginative, charismatic, and the best bullshitter on the island. He should have been a *picador*, a Spanish playboy, all his life and not got trapped into marriage and parenthood. All the different personas he invented to get laid covered the insecure brute that lay inside. But I never liked those staring pale-blue eyes, and neither did you. There was a madness in them that soon revealed itself when I became his possession and obsession.

Why didn't I pay attention to that first intuition? The truth is that I stayed in Mallorca and tried to keep my head above turbulent waters, whilst you returned to England. At times neither of us could believe what happened during those unhappy years, nor his tragic death. But the nightmare also brought forth two sons, four grandchildren, and a way of life I could not now give up.

Thank you for being there for me always.

I love you,

Elspeth

***

I walked to the village post office, which still maintained its grey stone façade and twee interior. Daffodils tossed in the cold March wind along the grassy banks and in all the gardens I passed on the way. They offered up different shades of yellow and white in generous clumps I was tempted to pick. But I resisted a habit I had often been scolded for in my childhood and just stood there with my sister's letter in my hand. It went back into my bag without a stamp. Then I wandered to the Norman church, a Grade II listed building where Caroline and I used to sing in the girls' choir. St Andrews smelt musty and damp from centuries of soft Devon rain seeping through the thick stone walls that were clammy and cold to the touch. It was full of unobtrusive art treasures I had been totally unaware of back then. All I could recall was my rosy-cheeked self in a blue cassock, trying to keep a straight face during the funerals and being prodded viciously by the choir mistress. I remembered feeling light and joyful most of the time, unaware of how happy I was despite the persistent colds and chilblains from playing outside in all weathers. That was before I was molested on the train, and I lost my cheekiness.

What was it about Devon and Somerset that converted it into my Garden of Eden? Then, the countryside stood tall about me, the grass so thick it could lacerate my bare legs as I strode through endless fields and sat on hilltops, surveying the soft green hills that were part of my kingdom. The bluebell woods were home to fairies hiding behind every tree, trees that awed me with their girth and height, the branches constantly creaking in the breeze. It was a land of red earth of unending possibility, full of harmless mysteries that reflected all the beauty and potential life had to offer. Then I knew nothing of malice, or lack of freedom. It was a time in my life when there were no filters between nature and me. I blended in effortlessly with it all, in a constant state of communion and unconscious connection. No need for meditation back then. I had never been so free, but now at seventy I had achieved another kind of freedom. It was freedom with a load of discernment that I carried on my back. I was free to go where I wanted, do as I pleased, contemplate or have fun doing nothing in particular. While my health held.

As the daughter of a stationmaster, railways and steam engines had been a source of fun and awe. Later, in Surrey, where electric trains had replaced the old beauties, my father more than once came home white-faced from the station in Redhill to tell my mother that someone else had jumped on the lines. For the inmates of the local mental hospital the frequent trains were the definite solution to their hell. It was the first time I had heard of suicide. Paradise lost.

Back in the B&B I packed my case, answered the WhatsApps to reassure my family and friends I was safe, and then drove to the station, where I left the rented car and boarded the slow train to London, back to King's Cross where my father finished his working days as stationmaster, the last one of five generations. Having two daughters finished that tradition.

I would have time to contemplate part of the precious scenery of the West Country as the train wound its way through Devon, Dorset and Somerset. I had to accept that some of the rolling hills and woodland now lay under motorways and housing estates. Time to say goodbye.

THREE

Knebworth, Herts

Monday 6 April

Dear Tom,

As you can see, I'm writing to you from Knebworth, that haven for outdoor pop concerts you loved so much. I have brought photos of all the holidays we spent here. I have a record of you from blond two-year-old playing in the front garden to a sulky fifteen-year-old leaning with style against the kitchen door. I nearly skipped coming here as I don't have the best memories of it; not because it isn't pleasant, green and leafy, a typical middle-class English village, and much better than the nondescript, grey concrete hell of Stevenage where your grandmother worked part-time in that dull electrical shop. It's because it was never home. The first house I only came to visit on holidays after Nanny and Grandad moved from Redhill after his promotion to King's Cross. But it was the first one where you got to know them and England. Then when they moved, you in your late teens and early twenties used to visit them at their final dwelling place in Seaford, back by the sea they had missed so much. You were always in search of the grounding and solace they gave. Except for you and your brother, the Knebworth era was a time of dissatisfaction for us all. Your grandfather retired here and was never himself after leaving the railway. It was as if he'd lost his identity. And Nanny's frustration and loneliness increased with every year they lived in the little cul-de-sac where hardly anyone passed by.

But I think for you it was your childhood paradise, just as Devon was for me. A momentary refuge. You ran free in the recreation field instead of being cooped up in small, cramped flats with scruffy doorways and entrance halls like dark tunnels. Above all you were free from your parents' unhappiness. No wonder you were wild, almost possessed at times. But maybe the time of my pregnancy with you also had something to do with that because I lived in a state of fear and homesickness. The terror of your father hitting me in the fourth month or constantly terrifying me with his fits of rage, must have affected you. How bad I feel about that, even now. Your twenty-year-old mother had no escape from that ancient world of madness, no barriers, no defence mechanism.

My parents were not the kind to say, 'We're coming to get you'; no, it was more a case of 'We're worried about you, but you've made your bed, you've burnt your boats, and we don't really want to be bothered by having you back here with a baby'. Not that they said it in so many words, but the message was clear. It had been bad enough with your aunt Caroline living with them after her separation. That was the beginning of her estrangement from them. It grew from a profound disappointment in realising they couldn't cope, that they were not able to give the depth of support she needed. Maybe I feared that too, subconsciously, and held on. How hard it is to perceive that your parents' love is not as pure and selfless as you thought. On the other hand, why should they have been burdened with the mistakes of their adult daughters? Responsibility for your children ends at some point, but we hope in the depths of our infantile souls that their unconditional love will still scoop us out of the mire and set us back on our feet again. My rational mind sees how unfair that is, but not my heart. That is something you are probably coming to terms with. We are responsible for ourselves, counsellors tell us, but it's a hard and lonely road to reach that level of freedom.

Of course, Nanny was your heroine and rightly so with her tolerant, laissez-faire attitude, house with large garden, and her efforts to entertain you and your brother. It was the magical month of August, and you always cried coming back on the plane to Mallorca. On arrival we would step into the damp heat as if we were being immersed in warm soup and immediately miss the fresh summer air of England. Tempers were frayed and you played up continuously. I understood later that your uncontrollable tantrums were your way of expressing your sorrow and confusion. That part of my heart will never be mended. It may have grown a scab, but it is easily knocked off.

As the eldest you witnessed the worst, although your hypersensitive brother no doubt was just as aware on a level beyond the physical. But you had direct access to the shouting, the threats, the long faces, your father slumped on the sofa for hours, chain-smoking, the devil staring through his eyes. And me hiding under the bed when his anger towards me boiled over. You were the first to warn me, when you were eighteen or nineteen of the other women that he must have brought home when I was in England; of the long, alien black hair stuck to the bathroom tiles, the smell of patchouli in the bedroom.

Then there was the confusion of the other extreme: the joking, the strutting, the boasting, the constant believable bullshitting. His influence on you was much greater than on your brother. The primeval power of firstborn over firstborn, as if you were his disciple, or had been in some previous life; the dark force glinting behind those staring blue eyes that pinned you down where he wanted you to be. Yes, how confused you must have been in your adolescence by his sermons advocating honesty and the alternating episodes of joviality and sick sexual jokes, then episodes of black depression. I remember him sitting at the kitchen table when he'd downed a few whiskies, asking you about your girlfriends, envy seeping through the words spat from his tight-lipped mouth:

'No double-dealing, now. If she's still a virgin, wait your time.'

'Only Prince Charles of England gets to marry a virgin nowadays.'

'I had two or three girls going on at the same time. Best days of my life.'

'Make sure you study and get a good job. You don't want to end up like me.'

You understood him the best. You understood the way he used his charisma to get what he wanted, the fear beneath the lies and the arrogance. You understood the desperate loneliness, how at bottom he despised himself and how he could arouse in us all a begrudging pity and compassion, just because he couldn't stop himself.

He was deep, wasn't he? He travelled through life like a submarine in dark seas, where all the debris lay. He could pick out the rubbish with his beam, but he could never clean it off, never rise to the surface where the light of day was. He thought he was clever enough to see the dirt others couldn't, that this was all life consisted of: survival of the fittest in the ditch.

Your father. You had to overcome him, integrate him, forgive him, admire what you could and somehow walk forward in life with that role model, your trembling psyche blanketed by your rebellious nature.

I used to sit at home with you as a baby and watch how he would put on one of his best suits (he bought two for the purpose) to go out for the night. I never knew where, probably to crawl the bars and discos for a pick-up. He would return in the early hours of the morning and give me a tender kiss on the cheek. I suppose it made him feel better. You were put into my arms when I was only twenty, an immature, scared, frustrated and deeply unhappy mother. As we all say, now I would do it differently, but you got the full brunt. I've tried to stop feeling guilty about it because the constant contrition, the not being able to change things, has made me ill. I tried to become Mallorcan so he would stop hounding me, but it didn't work. How could it? I submerged half of myself in the process. Or rather, was it that I gave pieces of myself away when I tried to fit in, when I squeezed myself into the straitjacket mentality of Mallorca in the 1970s? It was no good having a pseudo-Mallorcan mother, was it?

I wasn't able to channel your wild creativity then. You did that yourself through music and the bands you formed. What could you have been without a bipolar father and a mostly scared, self-lacerating mother? But you haven't done too badly. You certainly had an abundance of raw material to draw from. Your talent has developed over the years, and you are an admired, respected and well-loved singer-songwriter. Some of your best songs are the ones inspired by your father and your need to understand and integrate his life and death. They are the most painful ones for me to listen to. But you have a poet's soul and a constant need to express your emotions and confusion through your art. You have no desire for possessions; you get by with little, just enough to allow you to write the next lyrics in relative comfort with your black cat on your lap. Eccentric, sentimental, funny, free-spirited, deep-thinking Tom. The world needs more like you. And it needs your music, your lyrics and timeless rhythms. You search for the truth and aren't afraid to face it and to tell it. You are much stronger than you think. Even when you hit rock-bottom, you rise up. You never give up. The three of us never give up.

One thing you can be sure of: through all the madness, you were loved. Your father loved you in his twisted way until the day of his death and still does on whatever plane he is now. And what kept me sane was my love for you and your brother. I grew up with you both by my side, making mistakes along the way and especially with you, my rebellious firstborn.

Te quiero,
Mamá

***

I wrote the letter to Tom sitting in my room in a cheap boarding house near the station. The stale carpet had a faint vinegary smell, and in the corners of the room there were little whirls of solidified dust mixed with traces of the previous occupants. The cream-coloured paint, which had been layered thick on the doors and anything resembling wood, gave off a sickly smell which reminded me of canteens and school dinners. It was a smell of English cheapness and lack of hygiene. But none of it bothered me. It was all I could afford anyway.

Soon I would be leaving this village famous for its open-air rock concerts. I didn't bother to visit Knebworth House, a Grade II listed building in beautiful grounds. I remembered it vaguely from a family excursion in the eighties. But I did wander through the old village, past the tennis courts and the recreation field where Tom and Sam had lapped up every minute of playing freely in fresh summer grass with Turner skies overhead. My heart was heavy as I remembered how little I could give of what they needed as children. Just two weeks, sometimes a month, in a year of otherwise living in a small flat high-wired with tension, in the middle of a noisy city.

And yet Tom had grown up to be a man whose mentor and best friend was an old woman who lived in dire poverty. She would sing in the streets of Barcelona for a few coins, and he would sit with her on the pavement, oblivious to what people thought, proud of her company and avid for her words of wisdom. She guided him through his worst crises during his first raw years in

Barcelona. She taught him to see what lay beyond the physical world, to believe in his art and to be a seeker of truth however tough that could become. Her death was one of his greatest sorrows.

I walked up to Nutfield Close, a turning off the main road where the tall trees formed a shady canopy over the pavement. I found the house in the cul-de-sac where my parents lived for about eleven years. I had spent the last three months of my pregnancy with Sam here as I tried to escape from the ever-enclosing madness of my life in Palma. He was born in Welwyn Garden City, where the nearest hospital was. He lived in this house for the first two weeks of his life before we were carted off by his father back to the furnace of Palma in August. I remembered Mum's tears and Tom's when we said goodbye at the airport after three months' peace in this unpretentious, temporary little haven.

I felt a quiet stillness as I stood in front of the semi-detached house. It still had the red front door and brass knocker, and the front garden was still well kept with neat flower beds containing symmetrically placed plants. Everything under control. Dad would have approved of its tidiness and lack of weeds, and of the quiet which drove Mum mad. No one was to be seen even now. I remembered three-year-old Tom standing there in his red shorts and blue T-shirt, wild blond hair and happy rosy face. He was leaning on a toy lawnmower, exultant and brimming with potential. That is how I want to remember him, how I wish it could still be; every new day a chance to recover that life force, as fresh as it was at the age of three without any baggage.

I silently thanked my parents, especially my mother, for giving them that space, that freedom to be carefree children during the month of August for at least ten or eleven years. It enabled them to see that there were other, lighter ways of living, that life was not one drama after another, that some people were tolerant of faults and could even laugh at them. Those summers sustained and nurtured the children. Most of all they gave them contrast, the possibility to compare and know that there were other ways to live and be.

Apart from the last months of my second pregnancy in this house, the summer holidays were always spent under the shadow of the return to Mallorca and Javier. My mother had to deal with the large sack of problems I deposited on her table and with her own guilt at having allowed me to marry a foreigner they knew nothing about at the age of nineteen. She had been taken in by his charming bunk just as Caroline and I had. But not my father. His words after meeting him were: 'He's a bullshitter.' But he signed the consent form for me to marry, allowed me to leave university, because he was afraid that I would turn against him if he refused. They were not strong enough. They were not passionate enough. They didn't rave and shout or bang their fists on the table. They acquiesced just in case they might be wrong. They were so English.

I had had enough of England for a while, even though spring had arrived with its exhilarating show of tender green leaves and gardens flowering in the soft English light; even though I had discovered bluebells in patches of woodland on my walks just outside the village. The spring hurt, England hurt, the way I saw myself all those years ago here in Knebworth hurt. I needed respite and distraction. I stayed a few more days in my smelly room, wandered a little more in the countryside, and then one morning packed my bags and got the train to London. From there I boarded the express train to Gatwick airport. I spent one night in a spotless, soulless beige room at the Travelodge and found myself missing the smells of the boarding house. Tom's letter remained next to my sister's in a corner of my travelling bag.

The next morning, I was on a plane going south to Italy.

FOUR

Florence

Saturday 2 May

Dear Marisol,

As you can see, I'm writing from Florence. I'm sitting in Caffé Rivoire, the one that looks onto the Piazza della Signoria. Do you remember? Of course you do. It was where we had our first overpriced meal. We had just arrived from the airport, dumped our suitcases in the hotel and set out to explore, although I could have rested on the bed for at least an hour to get my dwindling energy back. We were still reasonably excited and well-disposed to each other, but I should have taken your imperious desire to do as much sightseeing and take as many photos as you could squeeze into those three days – preferably of yourself next to the right monument – as an ominous sign of what was to come. I took the first photo of you posing under the replica of the statue of David in front of the Palazzo Vecchio, which you weren't that interested in visiting.

There aren't as many people here as there were that jam-packed May bank holiday two years ago, nor is it the stifling twenty-eight degrees that we sweated through in jeans and jumpers; or rather I did, as you dressed in your usual daytime uniform: black designer jeans or leggings and T-shirts, over which you wore a variety of colourful lightweight jackets. I'll never forget you teetering along at surprising speed in six-inch stacked-heel boots, even up and down the vertiginous stairways, me panting behind you. The people I see strolling in the Piazza or sitting in the café are mainly wealthy-looking Italians parading their finery, showing off *la bella figura* to all who want to look and casting a critical eye over the competition. This piazza is the heart of Florentine social life, just in the style you like and so similar to the Mallorcan one, though on a minor scale, of course. You would fit in well here.

What happened on that trip was a turning point in our relationship as sisters-in-law and in our kind of friendship. I say 'kind of' because there was never total sincerity, was there? Although there was certainly affection, even love built up over many years, from when we were two young girls of fifteen and nineteen. But our first trip together, and probably the last for years to come, brought to a head all that irritated me about you. And probably all that irritated you about me. The fact that I was exhausted by three days of an organised trip of twelve-hour excursions didn't help my mood. Hours and hours on a coach driving through the Tuscan countryside, a quick visit to Siena and Pisa, then the Cinque Terre on those overcrowded little trains. We were shunted backwards and forwards, herded with all the other tired tourists trying to savour some of the beautiful places invaded by us and previous hordes of mass tourism. I would have been content with less just to have had the time to contemplate, to let it seep into my bones and bring back an indelible memory of smell and colour and sacred buildings. That wasn't your fault, of course. You wanted to see it all, skim the surface of everything on offer, to be able to say you had done it, and you brought back trophies to prove it. You had the energy and will to get your money's worth. And I was to be your faithful *escudero*, your squire. And as usual, I didn't say what I really wanted.

I was exhausted not only by the trip but by your bossiness and egocentrism, as if you were some Babylonian queen around whom everyone must run circles and grant her every wish. I was tired of the continual 'Elspeth, can you bring me this?' 'Elspeth take another photo; I don't like the way I look in this one.' 'Let's go to this restaurant.' 'I don't want to eat these sandwiches.' 'What do you mean, it's too expensive?' '*¿Qué te pasa,* Elspeth? You're always tired.' 'Elspeth, I'm getting wet. I need more of the umbrella.' Et cetera. There was also the question of my tight budget compared to your non-existent one. Money flowed for you; any whim was satisfied on the spot. You were, are, Miss Consumer. But now, looking back, I wonder if that nervous scratching of the surface of things, the unending search for instant gratification, for shallow delight, was not a covering up of unrecognised depression and sadness. You could not or were not ready to sit in unmoving, challenging silence and listen to what your soul was whispering to you, to face your truth. Who were you now without your husband, what could fill your emptiness, give meaning to your life when all that was left to you was the cold comfort of money? We both need to look into our private chasms, stare without blinking at the sorrow and joy of our lives. For only then do we own our lives; only then comes peace and wholeness.

But because you were still bouncing on the surface of things, I could only see the negative in you on that trip: your vanity, your constant need to be the most powerful, the most beautiful, the richest, the BEST. Italy lost part of its charm under the onslaught of your energetic narcissism. But partly that was my fault. I was the one who was changing, feeling inner stirrings, the lost pieces of myself striving to be recognised. Because that's what happens when we try to fit in for too long; we lose parts of ourselves. I no longer wanted to pander to your whims, make your life easier, be a shoulder to cry on. I no longer wanted to be a doormat with a grudge. At times I could have slapped you, or told you to fuck off, told you that what I was seeing reminded me of Javier, the emptiness under the posturing, your egos like balloons filled to bursting, bouncing over your heads. But we pay a price for everything, don't you think? And I had paid the price for being too amenable, too much a people-pleaser, partly to be accepted into this foreign culture, partly to like this new version of myself. So, in the end, I only have myself to blame.

You'll be wondering, if you haven't already torn this letter up, why I've come back here. I want to feel, see, hear and smell what I couldn't two years ago. I want to wander at my own pace and let the centuries of this beautiful city roll over me. I want to rediscover the magic of Florence that I felt when I visited it at the age of sixteen. I want to convince myself that I can still find it after more than fifty years. But also, I want to think about you and the roles we have played in each other's lives and how I allowed myself to become such a dedicated player. And I think I owe you an explanation of why I distanced myself from you after the trip. You'll hate me for my honesty, you who could never bear the blunt truth, who has cupboards full of family skeletons because what matters most for you is your honour, what others think of you, even though the shining image is built on a foundation of fiction.

You have the full right to tell me exactly what you think of me; in fact, I would welcome it. This is a time for clearing debts, for getting rid of nasty old cobwebs spun by fat spiders. It's time to show ourselves as we truly are with all our defects and virtues. I can't live with half-truths anymore, with barely covered envy and mean little jealousies. God help us if I ever shone more than you. But going back to the trip, you no doubt thought I was a pain in the ass with my tiredness, my silence and half-concealed black looks when you always grabbed the menu first and always ordered first in any restaurant we went to. People, even friends and family, have to be of use to you. I think my usefulness went down quite a few notches on that trip. Imagine how glad I feel about that! You probably felt quite confused about my behaviour and criticised me ferociously to your daughters when you got back. You may have wondered what you did to upset me after a few months of no communication, but the fault would always lay heavily on my side. I had broken a pattern, a role, and you had nothing to take its place. Maybe you felt scared, although you would never admit it. Maybe that trip was a mirror we both needed to look into. We have been wary of each other ever since.

But now I've had my long-needed rant, and I've declared that from now on I am myself, including the not-so-nice bits, I want to think about how much my story has been interwoven with yours, or if indeed we are our stories. We drag them with us, but they are not us. What I connect to isn't your story; it's you, when you are authentic. It's the fifteen-year-old I made friends with when I first went into that weird Mallorcan family fifty years ago, the girl who accepted me with all my English awkwardness at being constantly scrutinised by your parents. Your mother cried in disappointment when Javier first brought me to meet them and told them we were going to marry; your father seemed more interested in my mini-skirt. I was *la extranjera*, the foreigner, with all the nuances the word conveyed at that time: woman of loose morals, invader of Mallorca, future fidelity to be mistrusted, and shocking feminist tendencies. Although gradually they accepted me, even grew fond of me as I did them. They made a space for me in their tight-knit family structure. Your mother later took care of me when I was ill for three months with hepatitis, when my own parents didn't come to visit for fear of contagion. They were capable of great acts of generosity. And they were one of the reasons I stayed in the family for so many years. For all their initial strangeness and prejudice, I grew loyal to them. They became part of my family, as you did, Marisol.

You were there as younger sister of three brothers, just home at the weekends from a nuns' boarding school and happy at the prospect at having another girl in the family. You didn't care if the family wondered if I was pregnant, had had other boyfriends or why Javier hadn't chosen a decent Mallorcan girl. You loved the novelty, the fact that I was different. You already did what you wanted by means of a thousand subterfuges to find cracks through the straitjacket of Mallorcan customs and morality. What happened to that girl? When did you start to change? When you were manoeuvred into marrying the wealthy, boring entrepreneur? When the constant brainwashing, drip by drip, finally sank in and the gods of money and status took their places on your fragile altar? Whenever you came home from visiting somewhere, your mother's first question was always '*¿Te han hecho caso?*' Did they take any notice of you? Because not to have been taken notice of was the worst possible offence, as if your very existence had not been recognised. That all-pervading sense of honour was a tough shield defending vulnerable egos, wasn't it? Not to have been taken notice of was almost as bad as being laughed at.

You could have been so much more. Your beauty, vitality, sense of humour and creativity needed another soil to flourish in, one that wasn't fenced in and sprayed with all kinds of pesticide; one that didn't produce stunted little flowers with no insects. You could have been a stunning wild bloom. But you adapted. You had no choice. You became a master of deceit, just as your mother and so many women had before you. Your conversion to the system was made relatively tempting. As the only girl in the family, you were 'carried on a golden plate', spoiled and protected by a doting mother, brought up to believe you were the best and deserved the best. How different to me, who was continually told not to get too big for her boots or 'Who do you think you are? We are just ordinary people', whenever my parents thought I might get big-headed.

And yet your generation saw the transition from forty years of dictatorship to democracy. There were stirrings of change and underground rebellion even in your childhood. In your first year at university in Barcelona you made a feeble attempt at freedom, you tinkered superficially with new ideas, even ran away from the *grises*, the grey-uniformed police, like every other student in those exhilarating pro-democracy demonstrations. But it didn't last long, did it? Who would want to sacrifice money and comfort to defend a few anti-fascist ideas? It was a game you played while you were a student, just to be one of the crowd and look cool. Back home, the weight of Mallorcan tradition always won over and stamped out any signs of change. But when you came back from Barcelona for the holidays you were lighter, fresher, more alive, with a different conversation. You had been made to think of other possibilities, and you had seen other ways of living in that avant-garde city. It didn't last for long, but I swear you were happier then, when you were at least giving yourself a chance to grow over the fence.

The role of Babylonian queen with adoring entourage that you invented is a cover-up for the loss of you, Marisol. And the trouble with believing the stories we make up is that someday they dissolve into thin air and there aren't even any torn pages left to pick up. Your husband dies, your daughters don't turn out the way you expected, your friends dwindle, et cetera, et cetera. You still try to be that queen, wandering alone in your tarnished palace, because that's all you can relate to. For the time being. But maybe sometime in the future, that creative other you will poke its head out of the undergrowth and produce something beautiful and meaningful for at least a few people. That's all we can aspire to leave behind: a little beauty and the love we've given others.

Because underneath this onslaught, and part of me knows I have no right to be criticising unless I've walked in your shoes, I'm hoping you'll come up for air and be you. I've glimpsed it in the odd painting you've done when you've overcome your laziness, when you stop competing and putting on airs. When your world crumbled through the death of your husband. Then you became a recluse, you only wanted your clan. You included me in your clan. Even when I left your brother, even when he died, I was still part of your clan. Underneath the petty rivalry and envy, you have loved me in your possessive, exclusive way. As I have you, beneath the irritation at you and myself for allowing this fiction to become epic. Now it's imploding. One of the characters has got out of hand.

But, yes, I have always been part of your clan, at least until now. You never turned your back on me when I ran away from Javier. When I was so unwell in those five difficult years after the separation, you came to sit with me even though you never lifted a finger (lesser mortals could do that). You needed me to be well for you, to support you, to be a mirror for you. Is that how a narcissist loves? But maybe I'm being unfair here. My distancing must have hurt you a lot. First you lose your husband and then your right-hand woman. I have become independent,

Marisol, but we haven't lost each other. It's time to let go of hypocrisy and pride and to be what we are, even though it doesn't always look nice. I don't want any other kind of friendship. Because there is a kind of cruelty in hypocrisy; there is a lack of love and respect. You can write me the nastiest letter if you like and tear me into little pieces. I would welcome it. But deep down I don't really care, because nothing you can tell me surprises me. I would like to have a sincere friendship in our old age, when our egos have shrunk from all life's beatings. It could be fun and refreshing to laugh at each other and ourselves, at all the ridiculous mistakes and stupidities of our younger years, for not being who we simply are.

Thank you for caring about me, for loving me a little underneath the competitiveness that's always been there and even when I refused to be your faithful squire. In the hard years of my marriage, especially at the beginning, you lightened up many hours of my life with your sense of humour and attractive frivolity. You were my introduction to Mallorca as much as Javier was. You were an eye-opener to the role of women, especially in the times of Franco and the transition. Through you I've witnessed how those women have evolved and grown stronger and stronger. You have been a very important part of my fifty years on Mallorca. This and the love I feel for you under the irritations and annoyance mean that perhaps we deserve another chance to rebuild our friendship.

Please forgive how much I have hurt you in this letter. I have no choice but to be truthful. It's your turn now.

Te quiero,

Elspeth

***

It took me two weeks to decide whether to post the letter to Marisol or not. I carried it with me in my bag as I roamed the streets of Florence, just happy to look at its beauty and rest when I got breathless. Mine would be a poor tourist's stay. I would walk to the places that were either free to enter or very cheap. I was staying in an inexpensive B&B, eating sandwiches and fruit during the day like the student I was in the sixties. What a glorious feeling of freedom took over me as I slowly dawdled my way around this grubby, sacred city with too much art, too much beauty for my senses to absorb at once. It had to be done bit by bit, in small doses, or not at all. Some days it was enough to sit in a café and listen to the birds twittering early in the morning or watch how the sunlight struck the buildings in patches of pink and gold. Because unusually for me, I was getting up early, sometimes as early as six a.m., to catch the silence that reigned over the sleeping city before the first sharp sounds of shutters being rolled up broke it so rudely.

On those delicious dawn walks I was often reminded of Palma and Barcelona. It was in the cry of the swifts that swooped over the Duomo, or the blackbirds nesting in the parks, the signs of May in southern latitudes, the celebrants of spring; in the seasonal fruit displayed in the Mercato Centrale, the first apricots and kumquats, the last strawberries; in the dirty side streets with overflowing rubbish containers that took up half the narrow pavement. But there was a solemn magnificence, an unfathomable mystery in Florence which imbued it with a magic I have only ever felt in one other city: Oxford. These are places I am always reluctant to leave however overcrowded or noisy, places where I always feel I am missing something, not grasping some underlying meaning, so I know I will return just to see if the veils will lift.

I walked along the banks of the river Arno up to the Ponte Vecchio, as I had with Marisol. This time I wasn't constantly jostled by the May bank holiday tourists or stopped to take yet another photo of her until she was satisfied that she looked slim enough and that her dyed blonde hair was still as straight and smooth as a broom head as when she had left the hotel. Now I could look at the grey-green waters and wonder how many feet had trampled this bridge since 1345, how foul-smelling it must have been centuries ago when the Black Death spread its terror along its banks. Now the medieval bridge is lined with shops selling gold and silver jewellery, blatantly touristy like part of the old quarter of Palma. I kept walking and found myself in a little neighbourhood where there were small artisan shops and cafés. I could have been in Barcelona or Palma yet again. But I didn't mind or even feel vaguely disappointed. I had little money to buy anything other than food and was content to drift and look and get lost.

The Duomo was my reference point when I did get lost. Normally I would have panicked, but the calm that came over me in this city was as strange to me as getting up at six in the morning and not putting on my make-up to face the world. I soon knew the streets that stretched from the Duomo to the Arno River. They were full of expensive clothing shops, restaurants and gelaterias. If I had had the money, I would have purchased some of those beautiful clothes. In that I understood Marisol so well. Maybe if I had been in her shoes, I too would have bought on a whim. It's hard to resist beauty in any form; and beauty is thrown at you, with aggressive ostentation and with subtle refinement, everywhere you go in Florence.

Very often I would take refuge from this aesthetic onslaught in the Botanical Gardens, in the *Jardín Secreto*, and just sit and daydream on a bench with the May sun warming my bones and dappling the luscious plant life. I would listen to other secret life forms buzzing in the bushes or making the leaves and grasses sway and rustle. All around me were delicate, interlaced systems of life that were so easily destroyed through ignorance, through simply not recognising them. And I couldn't help thinking how often we blindly stamp on each other.

Sometimes I would bask in a mindless stupor like a cat stretched out, belly upwards, trusting and vigilant; other times I would think of Marisol and the Mallorca I had seen through her eyes and how I imagined she had seen me. But in those moments, I was an onlooker of that life with a detachment that would have made my yoga teacher proud. I wondered at the naïveté of the young woman who at the height of her physical and mental capacity had allowed herself to play such a self-crippling role. But it seemed the only way she could survive the weight of shame and fear. The taking on of a self-effacing role of humility and sacrifice was an endless act of contrition for what I could never be. Javier stood on the shoulders of generations of Mallorcans for whom male chauvinism was as normal as the eldest son inheriting the best piece of land. It simply was as it was. But I had come from a different place. I had no excuse for accepting the unacceptable.

After two weeks of wandering and watching, of dreaming and thinking, I decided to post the letter to her. I walked up to Piazzale Michelangelo, a large square on the top of a hill from where I had panoramic views of Florence. I panted up the steps leading to the top and dropped into the nearest café. There was another replica of the David in the square and the usual vendors. Suddenly I felt I had had enough, that it was time to move on. I drank my cappuccino, took out the crumpled letter from my bag and bought a stamp in a souvenir shop where I was served by the first blue-eyed, black-haired, handsome Florentine I had seen in two weeks. As I walked to the post box in the Piazzale, I wondered how many more there were like him hidden away in dingy little family businesses instead of parading themselves for ageing women to ogle at and brighten their days.

But when I was about to post the letter, I stopped. The thought of her reaction brought with it a stream of memories of Marisol and those first ten years or so of living in Mallorca when I was under the wheels of fear and contrition. I remembered her warm acceptance of me and, later on, how she stood by my side even when Javier died. I had allowed myself to be her right-hand woman in my constant need for acceptance, in my incapacity to say 'no'. My illness was already revealing itself in that trip to Italy and my tiredness was manifested in irritation at her bossiness. She was a product of her family and culture. What right did I have? I would send her a postcard of the statue of David instead.

The fact is that I was also fascinated by this family rooted in millennial traditions, who were so solid, so sure of themselves in their unflinching beliefs. Mallorca was the centre of the world to them; anything or anybody outside the island was inferior, second-hand, under instant suspicion. The world I had come from seemed flimsy and insecure in comparison. Even the walls of the houses seemed thicker, more resilient, with a character of their own. They were alive. The houses I had lived in were unsubstantial, empty shells when stripped of their furniture, just like any other along the street, and easily blown away. I had moved five times in the nineteen years I lived in England; in Mallorca people hardly ever moved – their houses were part of them, impregnated with their suffering and joys, passed from generation to generation and the source of constant inheritance wars among siblings.

Parents did not expect their children to become independent at eighteen; they were fiercely protective of them. I came to understand what family life meant in Mallorca, with all its tragedies and dramas. Families were clans. They stuck together, even though they fought day and night. The lack of a civic sense was covered by a profound sense of family. It was the opposite to what I had experienced in England, where children were often felt to be a nuisance, but you did your duty as a good member of society; you paid your taxes and kept as quiet as possible except for Saturday nights at the pub, where after a few pints you were officially allowed to let your inhibitions run wild.

In that raucous Mallorcan household, easy-come emotions often escalated into high drama. Situations were lived with such intensity that in my first year there I began to think that my life had been passionless and dull. The constant outbursts of shouting, where language was used as a weapon to be dodged and counteracted, not to communicate and understand, exhausted and confused me. Nobody seemed to listen to anyone, but as quickly as the storm had brewed, it was over. On the other hand, serious arguments could go on for days, with my feral father-in-law banging his bald head against the wall and my mother-in-law either in floods of tears or brooding over some sneaky revenge. It was all she could do with a violent husband who in a rage once broke a chair over her head, who would thrust his younger children's faces into their dinner plates if they wouldn't finish a meal. How well I came to interpret my mother-in-law's warning sentence: '*Cuidado, está nervioso. Hazle caso*'. Paying attention to him, acknowledging the man in the beast when we arrived, seemed to placate the devil in him. If anyone could have been a role model for Jekyll and Hyde, it was him. He was either prostrate on the church floor, arms outstretched in penance and giving speeches on God and morality, or he was ranting at home or at the neighbours about some imagined injustice. His bald head was never free of scabs. As soon as one healed, another took its place.

My mother-in-law, Doña Antonia, died at the age of sixty-six from bowel cancer, which nobody detected in time to save her life. She was small and dark with the face of a Madonna in her wedding photos, but over the years she became an overweight sallow blonde, and the corners of her mouth were turned down permanently, even when she tried to smile. She was uneducated, a good cook, and she loved money. Maybe it was due to the scarcity suffered in the Civil War, but every centime was counted in that house. Don Pedro, *El Viejo,* the old man, married her for her beauty and for the land her mother owned. I came to love and respect her in her struggle to survive in that surreal environment. In spite of her initial rejection of me for being *extranjera,* she was the first to encourage me to work and study, and vicariously enjoyed me being a *profesora* earning my own wages. Her long illness and death affected me profoundly and I wished I could have alleviated her suffering. She was more of an ally than I realised back then and wherever she is now, I send her my love and gratitude. Doña Antonia deserved a better and much longer life than the one she was allotted.

She relished telling her family that she was wilful and haughty during her chaperoned courtship, but *El Viejo* made sure to punish her for her short-lived upper hand after their marriage. As a child Javier often witnessed his father's fits of rage, saw him twist his mother's arm until it nearly broke and then go off to mass. I remember her saying to him in front of us all: 'Better to have become a whore than marry you.' There was a shocked silence after that.

But she survived on deceit. Her children often laughed at how she would listen outside the confessional when Don Pedro was asking for absolution from the priest for some of his sins. She knew, they knew, that he never confessed them all, but it gave her a little sneaky power. That was long ago when he still went to mass every Sunday, before he relapsed in his old age. She made her children her confidants and isolated him from his family. That was her revenge, and I couldn't help but forgive her. She milked as much money as she could out of him and hated to part with it. But *El Viejo* wasn't mean. He was too mad to be mean. When Javier needed money, he asked his father. But he learned how to deceive from his mother.

Laughter was also hysterical, high-pitched and contagious, at least to them. Conversations were usually monologues, always loud and grating. I lived in a permanent state of exhaustion. My head, my eardrums, my throat were sore just in the effort to keep up with them. How stupid I often felt and must have seemed in that first year, in which my imperfect Spanish and practically non-existent Mallorcan, a variant of the Catalonian language, prevented me from expressing what I felt. I realised how important language is to express who you are, where you come from, your whole cultural background. I had to break not only their linguistic code but also their cultural one. No one would make the effort to break mine to see who I was behind the label of young female foreigner, 'not one of us'. The loneliness of that linguistic and cultural isolation made me create a new persona, so desperate was I to fit in and be accepted. The miniskirts got longer, and my manners more submissive. The English and philosophy student went undercover. I was to be the perfect Mallorcan housewife.

This attempt at transformation was also brought about by Javier's jealous hounding. He was convinced that as I had slept with a couple of boyfriends before him, he was in danger of being a cuckold before the year was over. If you were not a virgin, you were a *putita*. Black or white. It hadn't occurred to him that he was worried about being deceived because he was the one who was cheating constantly and so imagined I was capable of doing the same. Utter madness supported by a male chauvinistic society in which the very language was full of misogynist terms and religious prejudice against women. I was treated as if I were not to be trusted, and I felt I was under constant vigilance. When I was pregnant with my first child and had the marks of the first blows of Javier on my back, he informed his father of 'my past' – '*tu pasado*' became his war cry over the years – and they both proceeded to discuss me and the situation. I was sitting between them on the sofa, so close I could smell my father-in-law's garlicky breath and the faint whiff of whiskey on my husband's. It was August, hot and humid, nerves were frayed as they always were in the intense heat, and Javier had pummelled out of me the details of my previous relationships. The father's conclusion was that 'as I was carrying a piece of his (Javier's) flesh, he should grit his teeth and bear it'. I slipped out of the room without them noticing, wondering how and when I could get away. Was Marisol ever aware of this? If she was, she never showed it.

Did their constant drama give meaning to their lives? Were all Mallorcan families like this? With time I discovered they weren't. There did also exist quieter, softer, more harmonious families in *la Isla de la Calma,* but at that time the majority were moulded by suspicion, the weight of iron tradition and closed-mindedness. The arrival of democracy and mass tourism gradually changed the mentality of the younger generations, but I had landed there in times when Franco was still revered as a demigod and any criticism of the system was regarded as a demonic tendency to be *rojo*, communist or socialist, an evil to be stamped out with self-righteous fury. Political attitudes were also black or white. Absolutes that had caused a civil war and a division that lasted decades. Most of the Spaniards of that time seemed unable to rise above that duality or at least build a bridge to connect to each other with tenuous shades of grey.

Some of Javier's generation were making timid incursions into new ways of thinking borne on winds from other European countries and from intermingling with tourists. What most attracted them was the idea of easier sex, not the political ideas. And here was born *El Picador*, the definition of which is: young male Spaniard, usually Balearic, whose main aim in life is to sleep with as many foreign girls as he is physically able to, whilst the formal fiancée, *La Novia*, stays at home to be kept pure for the wedding day. The prestige of *El Picador* rises with the number of tourists or foreign girls he has deceived with false promises and then had sex with. Much bragging, boasting and making fun of the fallen victim are also fundamental characteristics of *El Picador*. The species gradually became extinct over the eighties and nineties and nowadays is sometimes a topic of conversation for nostalgic old men.

Some *Picadores* did of course fall for their victims and end up marrying them, which was in most cases, although not all, a monumental mistake. Because even though *El Picador* appeared to be moving with the times and had a glossy veneer of modernity with his trendy clothes and Beatles hairstyle, underneath he was still an archaic Balearic who expected his wife to keep her virginity for him, to stay at home and look after the children and generally be *el reposo del guerrero*, the warrior's leisure, just like his mother had been. And here begins the tragedy. The foreign wife is usually neither a virgin, nor does she want to stay at home for the rest of her life when she is more educated than her husband and has been brought up to be independent. The poor *ex-picador* at first attempts to sublimate his rage, misery, and most of all his hurt pride at having married a sub-standard woman, by insulting her, sometimes giving her a shove or two, and when the first baby arrives, he dusts off his *picador* suit and hits the town again to see what he can find to heal his wounded self-esteem.

It is an even greater tragedy when there are still feelings of love which fight with the macho mentality and behaviour instilled from birth. In the same way as future alcoholics were raised at family tables by being given wine watered down with soda in their childhood, so were male chauvinists, as conversations about what a 'decent woman is like' were dripped slowly into their vulnerable psyches. But in these cases, where love confronts indoctrination, he knows in some untouched corner of his soul that he is wrong, knows he is destroying something precious. There is no use confronting him with the fact of double morality: men can do what they like, sleep with as many women they like, be adulterers and be admired for their manliness, whereas women are considered sluts, *putitas,* if they have a few partners. He will just reply,

'That's the way it is. Men spray, women are stained.' And so, both partners wither, love becomes a tortured caricature of what it once was, lives are lost or mummified. That was us; that was Javier and Elspeth, who couldn't escape each other, or save each other.

That was decades ago in another world. Now Mallorcan society is as free and easy, promiscuous and tolerant as any other European one, even more so in many cases. Sometimes, in the villages in the heart of the island, you get a whiff of how it was fifty or sixty years back, but mostly the old traditions have mellowed to ones of great hospitality and laissez-faire. It is no longer the indolent *Isla de la Calma*, prone to contemplating its navel and what the neighbours are doing. Now it's a dynamic money-making machine, full of ideas for improving the tourist trade it lives on, but aware too of how important it is to preserve its beauty and idiosyncrasies. The old fashioned Mallorcan is a species in danger of extinction, although they are still to be found in some of the *pueblos*. The Mallorcan language is more widely used and protected than it ever was in Franco's time when children were obliged to speak Castilian Spanish at school, but many Mallorcans have sold their land and heritage to wealthy foreigners. Tourists are the new invaders, and the island has been conquered by money. Now no one cares about sexual honour or what streets you walk down. Marisol's daughters can have all the partners they want and never set foot inside a church. I wonder how Javier would see his beloved island now.

Where would I go next? As I thought about the seventies and my struggle to adapt and ditch part of myself, a *forastera*, a mainland Spaniard, came to mind: the Andalusian María Consuelo. My next stop would be Seville.

FIVE

Seville

Monday 22 June

Dear María Consuelo,

Whenever I think of Southern Spain, which before mass tourism began was the stereotype of all Spain for the ignorant Brits, you come to mind. Here I am in the heart of Andalusia, in beautiful Seville. I know you are from Malaga, but Seville is the one city I was able to visit in the south and I never had my fill of its exquisite otherness, so back I came to think about the Spain outside Mallorca, and about ambiguous you.

You are probably still talking about the madness of *la inglesa*, in that closed-mouth way of yours so the words are squeezed out and only half heard by the unaccustomed listener. You never did quite understand my foreignness, my independent spirit straining to get some air beneath my self-imposed new identity. But then again, I never gave you all the details of my unhappy married life even though you tried to pry them out of me with subtle probing. I wasn't going to fall into that trap again; total honesty has only brought me great sorrow, not the lightening of burdens the self-help books tell you about.

We probably would never have become friends if we hadn't walked through the school gates together that September in 1977. It was our first day as teachers and we soon became confidants, pouring out our fears and frustrations to each other, comparing notes on how we were treated by the other teachers and *el director*. You'll remember how I used to drive you home most days and my car became a *confesionario* – of what we wanted to confess, at least. The roles were a bit lopsided because it was nearly always you who acted as priest. But, as you once told me, I also held up a mirror to you. We were, are, so different. You are ten years older than me, but back then it was as if the gap was twenty years. I remember you with your Marilyn Monroe hair and shrewd eyes. But you dressed as my mother would have, in smart, classical clothes; always knee-length skirts, never in jeans or trousers, your necklines always modest, just a slick of lipstick. You were the epitome of the respectable Spanish woman; a devout Catholic whose faith was the mainstay of her life. I wonder how you saw me with my gamine haircut, smoky eye make-up and hoop earrings. The miniskirts had gone but my clothes were anything but classical. I was tall and thin and for a short time looked younger than my age; you were small, rounded and your demeanour made you appear older than your thirty-seven years, although now from the perspective of my seventy years I would see you as a young woman. Ours was an incongruent friendship born of necessity.

We were both outsiders, both aliens to Mallorcan society, weren't we? You even more so than me. A mainland Spaniard was a *forastero*, a stranger, an intruder; a foreigner was a novelty as long as they minded their own business and brought money to the island. I think it took you longer than me to adapt to the closed society of the island, even though you had married a Mallorcan. You are open, friendly, witty and not too mindful of other people's barriers. You have stepped on quite a few toes in your time with your vitriolic tongue and direct manner. But that's what I liked about you: your warm-hearted generosity and sense of humour. Through you I came to know another part of Spain, one full of contradictions in its passionate radicalism, either right-wing Catholic or anti-clerical left wing. Either way, nothing was half-hearted; everything was done with desperate conviction.

Your Catholicism and faith fascinated me. Remember all those conversations about God and religious experience? It has occurred to me that subconsciously you were a link to my childhood encounter with the mysteries of being Catholic; you were the adult version of my seven-year-old friend with whom I made altars on the mantelpiece in my bedroom; you were the continuation of the symbolism and ritual that held some profound meaning I was not supposed to pry into. Protestants, Anglicans in their simple, neat, unadorned churches, seemed so dull, so tame in comparison to all this baroque exuberance. The incense, the statues, the flowers, the religious paintings, the solemnity of the mass in the dark churches overwhelmed and delighted me. Maybe it was more the aesthetics, more the form than the content, but its beauty and your sincere eloquence at one point had me on the verge of converting, of actually becoming a Catholic. I think you also had that hope, although you never said so outright, and I suppose you were disappointed when I veered off the path of traditional religious practice over the years.

I suppose also that you were the model of an upright Spanish woman who I could learn from, and above all in whom I could begin to understand a mentality in many ways so different to my own. Yours was a life of sacrifice and striving to live up to ideals. So, you put up with an unhappy marriage, with a husband who bored you to tears, and took your revenge in bitter irony and scathing comments. Many have withered under your cutting remarks or felt themselves to be plain stupid in the presence of your arrogant superiority. But then you would compensate with acts of kindness and generosity few were capable of. Your faith sustained and still sustains you, but it has never removed the anguish in your eyes, nor saved you from well-concealed depression.

I think life has disappointed you generally and I am probably on the long list of your disappointments. How could you see the whole me if you had no idea of what it was like to be a teenager in the sixties in the UK, to be influenced by the hippy movement at university, to have parents who let you do more or less what you wanted, as long as you didn't worry them too much? If you couldn't understand a word of English, had no idea of my culture apart from preconceived ideas and what you had studied in your history books about the Industrial Revolution and Protestantism? Ours was, is, a friendship based on effort, not ease. I grew tired of that effort, tired of not showing who I really am, of being careful not to make the 'wrong' remark about politics, homosexuals or feminism; tired of the caustic expression in your eyes and the tone of superiority in your replies because *la tonta de la inglesa*, the silly little English girl, was either too stupid to understand the truth or had strayed from the path of righteousness. Maybe it was difficult to make me out, seeing as I am a bit of an eclectic. Because I know my left-wing tendencies for social justice and social welfare clash with my more conservative spiritual beliefs that need constant watering. María Consuelo, I am all for gay rights and gay marriages, for the equality of women on all levels. I hate racism and exploitation of the weak and more vulnerable. How could I not? You are a staunch Catholic who covers her mouth in horror at the liberties of modern society. And yet your heart is generous. You are deeply compassionate. You cared for me during my times of ill health. You were the leader of a battalion of helping friends during those bleak hospital days. You did all you could for me. Did I not repay you with sufficient gratitude? Were you expecting another kind of friendship after that? You are eighty now. I think at one point, in the early years of our friendship when I was still very frightened and submissive, you imagined I was going to be the easy-going, unobtrusive friend you could lean on in your old age. But I became too independent, didn't I? After the separation I gradually recovered myself, and maybe you weren't so keen on that less pious version.

I must mention the phone calls. They were very hurtful. You tend to leave the mobile on after a conversation and so I could hear the comments you made to your husband. They were quite bitchy, María Consuelo. The worst one was when I rang you to wish you a happy saint's day.

You were at the airport waiting to take a plane to Malaga. As usual your husband answered and called you. Before you took the mobile, I heard you say quite distinctly, '*Qué quiere esa perra ahora?*' Well, the bitch in question just wanted to wish you a happy saint's day. You really should be careful of modern technology, María Consuelo. Part of me prefers to think that maybe you were referring to someone else, and if you weren't, I've forgiven you anyway. I'm still confused as to whether I didn't repay your kindness with the intensity you felt you deserved. Or maybe I haven't contacted you enough over the years? If that is the case, I will do my best to make it up to you. But even now, part of you is still a mystery to me; part of me still cannot reconcile your spontaneous generosity and warmth with the sharp sting of those acid remarks.

We still meet occasionally in the cafeteria of El Corte Inglés, don't we? We never talk about Javier's death now. *Para qué?* You are curious to know what I'm up to, to find out if I have a boyfriend. I wonder if for you I still carry the stigma of *la extranjera* of 'loose morals' who always has to have a man? Nothing could be further from the truth. My sixteen years as a single, separated woman have been one of a delicious solitude where the flag of independence flies high. Not that I haven't daydreamed about some wonderful, highly evolved man who could be my loving companion in the last years of my life, each respecting the other's vital process. It's all or nothing for me. At the moment, it's blessed nothing. And with the time left to me, what would be the point?

I used to wish you understood me better, that I could really open my heart to you without feeling cautious or just shy. You had to be me to know what it felt like to try and express yourself in a foreign language full of misogynist terms and religious prejudice. But I've gone past that now. I don't care anymore. You played an important part in my working life, and I like to think I also helped you in some ways. I'm a good listener and a willing chauffeur. Friendships move on and so have we. And with you I have had to ask myself if pure friendship exists, or what friendship actually is. I've come to the conclusion that friendship, as a form of love, arises from sharing your deepest sorrows as well as your joy. Whoever you share your suffering with, you love. Maybe we love in varying degrees of intensity depending on the level of our sincerity, depending on how much we share our soul journey with that person and on how much we do not feel judged. But a perfect friendship would have its downside because perfection leaves no room for growth or evolution; perfection is also stagnation. So, let's move on with all our errors, let's try another way.

What I'm most grateful to you for, apart from your many kindnesses to me, is that you helped me understand what part of Spain was like, what role Spanish women were supposed to play in that time and what I could never be. After some years that knowledge made me immensely grateful for the upbringing and education I received in England, for the freedom and open-mindedness I experienced there. It lay squashed and dormant for too many years but finally put out feelers, even at the expense of dire circumstances and suffering.

Even so, now and then I am saddened by your 'underground' remarks when your darker side arises, when you imagine yourself to be in the privacy of your home or just surrounded by your inner circle. What happens to your lofty Christian ideals in those moments? Strangely enough I don't feel anger or surprise, perhaps because I always knew that part of you was lurking underneath and could see how the 'beast' was coming up for air in your ferocious sarcasm. You can be a subtle bully. More than hurt, I felt guilt. How far had I strayed from the idea you had formed of me in those first years of our friendship? Had you expected a sisterly relationship where you would guide me along the path of righteousness in exchange for unconditional support and undying loyalty from me? I could no longer be that humble, pious version of myself. Maybe I thought you wouldn't approve of who I really am, have become in these sixteen years of independence and freedom. Maybe that is why I didn't contact you so often or avoided those probing questionings in the car or cafeterias where respectable middle-aged ladies met and discussed the world. I thought you would misjudge me, misunderstand me with your prejudice. Maybe I feared your judgement while I was still learning to be myself, my vulnerable self. Because I could see myself in your eyes, and the disapproval was also a reflection of Javier's despising. You belonged to the same world. I had tried to enter that world, be what he would have wanted me to be, through watching you. I realise this now. Back then, I only knew I had to survive through adaptation. Does this mean that I used you, if subconsciously? My God, I hope not. Was this the reason for those remarks? Were you deeply hurt by my change, and I didn't even realise? Were you more attached to me than I could have imagined?

Does becoming independent imply also becoming more selfish?

Before either of us dies, María Consuelo, I would like to have a conversation with you that lasts days or weeks, in some beautiful location away from the cafeteria of El Corte Inglés, where we both drop our masks and show our naked souls to each other, where the affection we both feel for each other can overcome prejudice and misconceived ideas. I think I may have been just as prejudiced as you appeared to me. Inside the person you know, there is someone you don't know, tucked away in a little chamber and too vulnerable to make an appearance. Maybe we could let each other have a respectful glimpse and not pass judgement.

Take this letter as one of gratitude and love for all the support you gave me in those flailing years of intense suffering and fear.

Te quiero,
Elspeth

***

At first I wandered around the streets of Seville with a heavy heart. Not even the white-gold light of those tall skies could shake me from a sense of how I had nurtured my own ego and licked my wounds after the separation from Javier and how I tried to load the weight of his death onto my overburdened back. But it was a flimsy ego that was easily knocked sideways by guilt and remorse. I had no choice but to burrow down in my little apartment and communicate less and less with people like María Consuelo, people who constantly reminded me of Javier and who probably in part sympathised with him although they would never admit it to my face. Nevertheless, I had formed a bond with María Consuelo in those first ten years, and I knew in my heart that she deserved an honest explanation of why that bond had slackened. She was now eighty. I liked to think that at eighty she had overcome many handicaps. On the other hand, they might have become more entrenched and for her the *imbeciles* and *tontos* of this world were increasing at an alarming rate. I had never heard anyone say the word *tonto* with more quiet venom than her. Most of us in her circle had felt like a stupid worm under that supercilious gaze, although we were never quite sure what we had done to deserve it. Such was her power. Yet her kindness to me and support in the worst moments of my life far outweigh the outbursts of spite and prejudice, unknowingly caused by my own lack of understanding of her need for recognition. Now from the perspective of age and illness, María Consuelo has been a unique friend who probably found me as difficult to fathom as I did her.

But the knots in my heart soon slackened and became undone under the *embrujo de Sevilla*. *Embrujo*, bewitchment, an adjective so often used to describe this southern city that it has become commonplace. Yet it was so apt, so beautifully fitting to convey the transformation that most people underwent when they set foot in this city. Was it the vast skies, white gold in the heat of midday, the onset of twilight – *el crepúsculo*, how I loved that word, – when the unequalled light gives way to a velvet profundity that makes even an atheist believe in the sacred? Or was it the mixture of Moorish and Spanish architecture, both ancient and fresh, the ochre, white, pink and turquoise buildings that sparkled along the riverbank? Or maybe it was the thirty centuries of history that whispered from the streets and the *plazas*, the churches and markets. It was surely all of this, but most of all it was an atmosphere of sensual indolence, of perfume and colour. In Seville, life has relaxed; burdens are lifted, and mine were too. Surely revolutions were not made here as they are in Barcelona or Bilbao. Differences of opinion would always be sorted over a glass of *fino* or fried prawns. The whole city was urging me to enjoy life, the moment, my failing body, the beauty around me. I walked along its streets with a constant smile on my face. Seville is not harsh or alienating as so many cities can be. It embraces you, pulls you into its innermost sanctum and then lets you go.

The *sevillanos* look different too. They are fine-boned and slightly built. They carry themselves proudly, straight-backed and gracefully dynamic. The wealthier ones wear beautiful clothes, but they wear them as a matter of fact, with *alegría*, not like the slightly snooty Florentines or Parisiennes. How could you not be in tune with this city of gold, ochre and white? How could you break that aesthetic harmony?

There is a vital energy in Seville that feeds on the beauty, the light and the smiling faces and manifests in a collective euphoria. This is the power of its *embrujo*, its enchantment. Here is a city where people are the protagonists. I watched people make friends in bars and laugh as if there were no tomorrow, and I too, as I wandered around the parks and squares, observing and imbibing this rotund, intense and positive way of living, began to recover an old, deep-rooted identity that just took joy in the fact of living, as a child would. I was rediscovering an innocence in myself. I was coming out of hiding. I could look, feel and enjoy without the filters of my overactive mind. The past faded away and I did not care too much about the future. I was here. I could breathe, taste good food, be chatted up by old *sevillanos* in centenarian bars who invited me to coffee, be dazzled by the cathedral and the parks and the Giralda, and, and, and … the possibilities were endless. Life was endless. I could do what I liked and be who I liked, and no one was judging me. Seville was life served on a golden platter with all the ingredients, and even at the age of seventy I could still taste it. But most importantly, I realised that my sixteen-year convalescence after the death of Javier had finally ended. My scars were part of me, and I was able to live with them and show them without any feeling of shame.

Back in my little *pension* in Triana, I thought of María Consuelo, chaperoned right up to her marriage, daughter of a strict military father and entrenched in her Andalusian roots; of the anguish at the back of her small brown eyes, of how much of her natural *alegría* she had repressed to adapt to Mallorcan society back in the sixties. We had both been exiles. She had never completely got over her homesickness for her native Malaga, but I had long stopped missing England. We had moved in different directions, but I owed it to her and to myself to have a long conversation with her when I finally returned home. I remembered our first encounter, she at thirty-seven, me at twenty-seven, when we walked through the school gates and asked each other if it was our first day. We leant on each other for support those first ten years or so. Because of that I will not post the letter to her from her beloved Andalusia, at least not for the time being. Maybe I will edit the harsh bits or leave them out altogether. She in her in her wisdom probably knows part of what I feel. And maybe it's better to leave a trail of gratitude and love for when my time comes.

Lying on my bed with its spotless white coverlet, the shutters opened onto an interior patio whose walls and corners were overloaded with pots of red geraniums and multicoloured petunias, I wallowed in a wonderful, unrepentant laziness. If I sat up, I would see the spectacle of the tiled courtyard, a cool oasis where the plants had just enough sunlight and water to become the maximum expression of their beauty. Just like the whole of Seville, everything, everybody could do nothing else but be the most splendorous versions of themselves, with seemingly no effort. I could no longer be the best physical version of myself. My thin blood was exhausted and red blotches had appeared on my legs, a sign I should be resting more. But I was not scared by this symptom and what it foreboded. I just continued to lie back and let thoughts gently cross my mind.

I remembered my previous three-day visit to Seville about twelve years ago. The school had sent me to an English language fair to get information and new ideas for the Trinity College oral exams I was running. It was March but already warm, and I rapidly shed my warm sweaters. After listening to a few of the boring talks from rival English language institutions, my sense of duty was fading as quickly as my interest, so I escaped as often as I could to savour a few of the wonders of Seville. I had been separated from Javier for about four years – he had died a year and a half after I left him – and for the first time I felt the weight of guilt lift from me as I walked the streets of central Seville. And in the first park I visited, El Parque de María Luisa, I felt free from the nightmare that had plagued me. More than the beautiful *glorietas* dedicated to the Machado brothers and Bécquer, what most delighted me were the ponds with ducks, the cypress trees and all the lush vegetation. There I felt I was part of something bigger than myself and my heavy baggage; there I felt the circular pull of the universe and how unimportant my sorrows were in this eternal dance.

I have a lot to thank my old school for. It obliged me to build a new version of myself: teacher of English as a foreign language. Not that I ever wanted to be a teacher. In my university days my ambitions were more sophisticated and romantic. I would become a journalist or a university lecturer, I would travel the world, et cetera, et cetera. It's quite laughable how blindly arrogant young people can be. At nineteen, little did I know that the future would knock me over. No, none of this was to be, but that school gave me work, financial independence, support and some good friends. Even so, the beginnings were not easy.

My first day at work was in September 1977. I had just recovered from hepatitis which had me in bed for three months. Although I had already lived in Mallorca for nearly eight years, this was the first time I was going to be plunged into working in a totally Mallorcan atmosphere that was still entrenched in Francoist ideas. And here began my friendship with María Consuelo, who was to teach ethics and history. It was the first time either of us had worked. We were both looked upon askance; she an outsider from the mainland, me a foreigner. I found out later that the rest of the staff had been warned by *el director* that an Anglican protestant was going to join the teaching body.

I remembered my first encounter with the students. I had youth and daring born of terror as I braved my way into the noisy classroom where thirty-five sweaty adolescents sat waiting to inspect me from head to toe. I thought I would scare the living daylights out of them by speaking to them in English and firing questions at the ones that looked most likely to cause trouble. This worked for the first ten minutes when they were shocked into silence by the first native English teacher they had ever had, but after a while they began to laugh and admitted they couldn't understand a word I was saying. As my name was unpronounceable to them, I was called 'la English'.

During that first class I was aware that I was being spied on by a lurking figure in the corridor. I later discovered that he was the Voice of his Master and deadly confidant of the headmaster, *el director*, who was a priest in name but looked and acted more like a ruthless businessman, and who had no qualms about cutting off heads if you didn't fit into the regime. The director also chain-smoked *Ducados* and had a horror of 'the Reds' taking over the government.

The spying on me, and others, continued for a few years. I never knew if the former *falangista*, the only fascist political party allowed in Franco's time, was checking to see if my foreignness – and therefore possible 'loose morals' – was going to contaminate the pupils, or if his repressed sexuality was getting a lift by having quick looks at my breasts and legs. We never did become work companions in all the years I taught there. His male chauvinism and unfair treatment of the pupils as he wielded his power in his little dark domain was too much for my independent upbringing, and even though I was under the wheels at home, I sometimes confronted him. He also knew Javier but had never been one of his friends. That was probably because he had never entered the *club de los picadores* and was later henpecked by his dominant wife at home.

My aura of 'foreign but manageable' also disappeared during the elections for the trade union reps at school. The dictatorial director was only allowing the one manipulable syndicate in his school; the alternative, more independent and progressive, was shunned as a possible nest of *rojos*, Reds. My burgeoning friendships belonged to this last one. I would probably have remained neutral and not voted for either of them had the director not summoned me into his office one afternoon and placed an envelope in my hand. What did it contain? The vote for the candidate who he was making sure would win. My vote went for the opposition, and I was no longer an enigma to anyone.

At times, the school also gave me a little social life. And for the first time since I had come to the oasis of Seville, as I lay on my bed with the sunlight flickering through the curtains, a horrible scene came to mind and woke me from my reverie: I was coming home from my first end-of-school-year dinner with the other teachers. It was midnight. A female colleague dropped me at the entrance to my block and drove off. As I stepped into the street I could feel Javier's eyes on me. I looked up to our sixth floor flat. He was leaning over the balcony, smoking and watching. My stomach was churning as I entered the building and went to press the lift button. But the creaking old lift was already coming down. When it reached ground floor Javier stepped out and pulled me in. I could smell the whiskey on his breath and the fear in his sweat.

'*Qué horas son éstas,¿eh?* Answer me, *puta*, answer me!' he said through gritted teeth.

I remembered him pushing me around the flat, his face inches from mine, the blue eyes unblinking, spitting out the same question ending in 'eh, eh?' When he stopped to light another cigarette, I quickly slid under the bed and lay there curled up in a ball. I hoped the children were asleep. I stayed there for hours, sobbing in the dark and the dust, until he calmed down. When I crawled out, he was contrite, ashamed. Until the next trigger.

How did I allow this to happen, year after year of psychological and sometimes physical damage? Overriding fear. Fear of losing the children, fear of utter loneliness, of having nowhere to go, of not being supported by my parents in England. I had burnt my boats, I thought. There was no going back. I was trapped. The new identity had to work if I was to survive. And that new identity could not describe to others how each day I lived not with a loving companion, but with an unstable adversary consumed by jealousy.

Thank God that at seventy I had come out of my hiding place and could embrace my idealised Seville. The ghost of my younger self could back off for a few more days here in this splendorous, generous city. Seville has a will of its own and it is no use trying to resist it. I had succumbed utterly. If I compare it to balancing the chakras, so in vogue now, then my second chakra was now a vibrant orange and whizzing at full speed. My sensuality had been nurtured; all my senses heightened. I could have drifted there indolently till I died, replete, in a whitewashed room that overlooked the Guadalquivir River. But I had to move on while my strength lasted. I knew I needed the whiplash of the north, the slap of cold winds, another kind of beauty. Oxford.

SIX

Oxford

Tuesday 7 July

Dear Alberto,

I'm writing this in my room in the bed and breakfast in Iffley Road, the same one I found for you to stay in when you came to visit me over four years ago. At night I can hear the owls hooting from the nearby nature reserve. Sometimes they intermingle with an ambulance siren on its way to the John Radcliffe hospital. The chaotic, dishevelled landlady is still there, her half-pissed, ex-punk Scottish husband lurking in the background. They didn't go with the quaint Olde English décor, the chintz curtains and flowery bedspreads, did they? But that was part of the attraction, imagining what they got up to in that pigsty of a back quarters they lived in. I was actually invited in there one day while she checked my bill on the computer. All my visitors ended up staying there so I suppose she thought I was 'of confidence'. You can imagine how pleased she was to see me again after four years. I've always thought the UK is a special breeding ground for eccentrics, and Oxford has an abundance of them. You see them everywhere, on buses, in the street, public libraries … you name it. The best thing is that nobody turns a hair.

I've been back to Parker Street and stood in front of the house, but I didn't have the courage to knock on the door. The little Edwardian terrace still has the advertisement for piano classes in the grubby window, the two bicycles are still leaning against the rubbish bins. How I suffered and loved that house. Hard to believe I spent a year there, living like a student in my narrow bedroom. You remember those luxurious Edwardian fireplaces in the rooms? You took photos of all of them when the landlord wasn't there. Mine was turquoise with elaborate carvings, and on the mantlepiece above were photos of my sons and grandchildren. I used to imagine them asking me what the hell I was doing there at my age, instead of supplying them with love and chocolate back home. You were impressed by that house, its beauty still intact from 1904 and even enhanced by the thick cobwebs that hung from the kitchen ceiling. There was just one threadbare carpet which covered the stairs in dusty patches, steadily being devoured by moths. Do you remember how the landlord gave me mothballs to stop them reaching my room and making holes in my clothes? I imagined an army of them marching under my doorway, the closest one to the stairs. He never did remove the carpet!

He was a strange, interesting combination of divorced Jew turned Buddhist, the sort you usually only find in cities like Oxford. I got used to his morning chants in the front room and the weekly communal ones. I even joined in a few in the end! They thought I was a potential convert, but it was more out of curiosity on my part, and I did find the chanting soothing. You met him once, I re-call, but not his daughters who were there only half the week. That was a challenge. Especially when my favourite black top went missing from the radiator in the bath-room, and they used up my shampoo and conditioner. But they were daddy's girls, and he believed their lies. Now I wonder how I put up with it all, the discomfort and some minor indignities like having to share the same bathroom with everyone. I would go up to have a bath and find one of the daughters sitting on the toilet with the door wide open, completely undisturbed by my appear-ance. Or they would forget to pull the chain, literally, on the ancient toilet and I would come across various shapes and sizes of submarines in the bowl. Maybe they wanted me, this old intruder, out of their home as soon as possi-ble. I think I must have been the first lodger to stick out the whole academic year in that house.

But their father was in dire straits financially and earned his living by giving endless piano lessons. In be-tween he would compose music for his next symphony. From the many friends and acquaintances who came to that house I learned that snobbery in Oxford wasn't rooted in what social class you belonged to or how much money you had; it was about how you were progressing in academia, or what new work of art you were painting, or writing or composing. The competition and jealousies were ruthless under the social niceties and witty conver-sations. My landlord wasn't so much worried about money as to how his symphony was coming along. Since I left, I read he had his concert for a string quartet per-formed at the Holywell Music Room.

But apart from minor inconveniences, like often being cold because the landlord only put the heating on at certain times of the day and having to use my bed as a sofa, I, we, loved Oxford. I was so pleased you came to see me that long weekend. It was December, the end of my first term, and you got up at dawn each day to walk along the paths that sparkled with frost in the winter sun all the way to Iffley Village to see the eleventh-century church, then along the canal that led to the centre, and through the wooded hill up to Headington. All of this before breakfast in that Hitchcockian bed and breakfast. Then we walked the streets of Oxford, and with you I again explored this city. We were always looking upwards, discovering new details, our senses a radar to new beauty and ancient buildings. We always knew how to awaken each other's sensibilities, didn't we? I miss the freshness and intensity of that first term. I constantly fought against the numbing force of becoming accustomed to the beauty and wonders that surround us, of not looking up and around to what habit makes us indifferent to. There was never any danger of that in your company. Your retina is larger and sharper than anyone else's I know. You have an artist's eye, even though you are a mathematician, and what you have seen and recorded of the world, all its colours, shapes, sounds and dimensions, would leave many agape if you had made a book of your singular journey.

Oxford reminds me of you, Alberto. Like you, it's stimulating, curious and brilliant. It's the triumph of mind, culture and effort, even to the point of overreaching itself to arrogance. It is the intellect stretched to breaking point, to madness, to the heights of those spires. Dear Alberto, you were the person who pushed me out of the bunker of my apathy and lethargy and brought back the desire to go forward into an uncertain future. With your often bitchy remarks that were like cruel little pinches or resounding smacks, you made me see I could still achieve so many things. And you made me laugh again, you made me feel silly and young and alive. You were one of the major steppingstones that led me to do a master's degree at the age of sixty-six, who encouraged me and then came to visit me. In those intense three days we talked endlessly over cream teas in ancient coffee shops in the High Street and walked in Christ Church Meadows, pointing at the nuances of colours in the sky and grass, or we just sauntered around the colleges, enjoying each other's company.

You have been one of my saviours, Alberto, another gift from the school we worked together in. You also stood by me when I had to flee Mallorca to escape from Javier, and at the time of his tragic death. You and other good friends have upheld me in the worst moments of my life; but you, especially, showed me I still had potential to live and learn, even though the vines, the thick creepers that bound me to Javier, should have been severed many years ago. Because work gradually became a refuge, somewhere to shelter inside the structured routine of classrooms, exam deadlines and often challenging adolescent pupils. The days rolled thickly into years of duties, the bubble of school life and the small pleasures within it. I had nothing else to get by. But as we got to know each other, going on the various school exchange trips together, I began to awaken from the role of sacrificial victim. I began to reinvent myself and slowly become the woman I was supposed to be, even though I had wasted many precious years. So much of it was done through laughter, through a way of lightening up the tragedies of life. That was an unrepayable gift. You hardly knew my story back then, but you intuited something in me that needed to be healed.

And being so much younger than my other friends, you were the break from the stifling traditions, still so full of prejudice, that lay festering under the veneer of modernity of many Mallorcans and Spaniards. You are the same generation as my own sons. You have travelled, studied abroad, read everything within reach. Your curiosity has pushed you from your island and made you realise it isn't the centre of the world, beautiful and precious as it may be. And yet, you never left. Even though you have been offered positions at universities abroad and have travelled to uncountable foreign lands, you have never uprooted yourself from Mallorca. You have brought your treasures home to pack into your bulging shelves and cabinets. What you have learned has been brought back to enrich other minds and to keep for yourself in your own private well of solitude. For we both know that all of us are alone in the deepest recesses of our heart. How we deal with that solitude is the mark of our creativity and sense of humour. You are a master of that.

And then, of course, we are both connected through our little vanities, our love of clothes and looking good, the love of beauty in general. Shopping with you was always exhilarating and exhausting, with me slumped in a chair while you tried on more and more outfits, or you appearing with armfuls of clothes 'that would really suit you'. You were usually right. And at school you were always the judge of our appearance: 'Have you combed your hair today?' 'You've got lipstick on your teeth.' 'You look like a lumberjack in that shirt.' 'Has the cat been sitting on you?' We would laugh but hastily take note.

Our trip down Cowley Road was a feast day for you with its charity shops and multicultural restaurants. You would have filled your case with second-hand books and Victorian china if you had had the space. It was supposed to be 'the street of a thousand restaurants' according to the guidebook, but it was much shorter and less glamorous than you imagined. I think you enjoyed its grubby, multi-ethnic charm far more than the patrician colleges that were just a stone's throw away. Cowley Road was life outside the academic bubble; it was the daily struggle to survive in the colourful, vibrant, dirty and noisy non-academic world where the dropouts and homeless took refuge next to the community centre with its endless exhibitions of students' artwork. Do you remember when we went to see the exhibition of the social sculpture students from Oxford Brookes? It was social denouncing or social awakening through art, which can interact with and transform society. It was a mind-stretching challenge to take part in those 'happenings' that I could only have experienced with you and your X-ray vision.

When you were tired of exploring, you listened with one ear to me describing what I was writing about on my creative writing course and to the descriptions of the people I met, whilst with the other you tried to catch snippets of conversation from people sitting at nearby tables in the pubs and cafés we went to. Then you would ask me what such-and-such expression meant, in your constant efforts to update your almost perfect English. You always had the capacity to do five things at once and do them all well.

Yours was a flying three-day visit in which I saw Oxford through your eyes and in which I was encouraged constantly to work on this course with its high demands and challenges. You were the echo of my mother's voice who said three days before she died: 'Make sure you do your best.' Never had I enjoyed or suffered more being out of my comfort zone, and never had I enjoyed more my freedom.

Dear Alberto, may you always be there with your wake-up pinches, your vision, your cutting sense of humour, your quest for beauty, and endless curiosity. You are unique, and although it sounds like a cliché, I am proud to be your friend,

Te quiero,

Elspeth

***

I had left the unfathomable skies and effortless rapture of Seville for the whip and spur of Oxford. But I could not recapture the intensity of the feelings and sensations I had experienced that year in Oxford. It had been unique, unrepeatable. However much I looked up at the power and beauty of Oxford's trees in full leafy bloom, the sycamores, the horse chestnuts, the willows, the cherries;

however much I wandered around the quadrangles of those lofty colleges of pale honey-coloured stone, I was no longer in awe, no longer regretting the fact that I had been offered the chance to study here when I was eighteen, and had turned it down because I didn't want to spend another year at school preparing the tough entrance exam. Instead, I had gone to Manchester University and left halfway through when I met Javier. I came full circle in that year, I journeyed back to my nineteen-year-old self, and it was enough. The ghost had been placated. The phantom of regret had dissipated.

One of my mother's regrets had also been lightened before she passed away only six months before I came to Oxford. She was the one who had most encouraged me and who was the most delighted when I told her the week before she died that I had been accepted at Oxford Brookes to do a master's degree in creative writing. But now the impetus was over. The people I had met were no longer here; nor did I have the focus of the course to hold me together in that avalanche of sensations, of newly awakened sensibilities that sometimes hurt, as if I were a disorientated teenager who had lost the soft padding of home. And they have stayed awake even as I go further into old age. What I learned through the knife-cutting edge of constructive criticism from the professors was exactly that; a knife that pared away the superfluous, sloppy thinking and writing, that put my battered little ego into a mirror for me to contemplate and then tell it to disappear. That year was pivotal, a turning point which I look back on with huge gratitude. It was also the realisation of the truth of Seamus Heaney's words, when he spoke of the 'angelical power of poetry' and of 'its function as an agent of possible transformation, of evolution towards that more radiant and generous life that the imagination desires'. I could apply his words to all the literature I read during that year.

Oxford was, is, food for mind and spirit, and for the senses. I listened again to the boys' choir in Magdalen College and once more was moved to tears by those voices. Who cannot believe in the sacred, at least for forty minutes, while listening to those cassocked false angels? I wandered down the narrow, cobbled lanes of old Oxford, retracing all the places I loved, the colleges where I could still feel the brush of ghosts slipping through the buildings and soaring up to the spires; the ghosts of choirboys who sang the madrigals every first of May from the bell tower of Magdalen College.

But even in this microcosmos of wealth, privilege and excellence there are still trails of suffering, of academic failure alongside the success of brilliant minds. Oxford has its dark side too. They were still there, the homeless and the dropouts, as I walked along Cornmarket Street, some of them so young they could well be students who had been knocked off the academic ladder and succumbed to the cocaine that was all too available for those who could not hold up under the pressure of achieving the excellence that was demanded. These are the victims, the true ghosts of academia and its ferocity, the Oxford that many avert their eyes to. When I was living here, I would give a few coins to a homeless guy who used to sit on the damp ground under the Saxon tower. Haggard and ragged, he would strum a dented guitar with red raw fingers in mid-January. For a few pence and in his private hell, he would sing over and over the first lines of Dylan's 'Knockin' on Heaven's Door'.

Now it was July, so the streets were packed, not with students from the colleges but with hordes of tourists and foreign language students who surged down the High Street in tsunamis. The shopping mall had been extended, and everywhere crowds surged like birds of prey looking for the best bargains, souvenirs or coffee shops. I needed to get away into the Meadows or down by the river Cherwell to find a quiet spot to listen to the boats creaking on the water and see the breeze ruffle the surface.

Rivers, any rivers – the majestic Guadalquivir running through Seville, the dreamy Cherwell, the tranquil Oxford canals with the ducks clustered by the banks, the murky Thames – nudge my soul out of its hiding place and expose my vulnerable heart. Sometimes when I watch them, I feel again the circular pull of the universe and I am lifted out of my inner world. I often dream of rivers, beautiful fast-running mountain streams or stagnated waters under dark bridges, if my emotional state evokes them. In the timeless and time-fraught year I spent here, many tears of joy and sorrow welled by these banks, especially the day I left. They were my moments of truth when the soul cannot be stilled. I had followed the river of my heart and could not stop its flow onwards away from Oxford and onto the next phase of my life, however short. Now I have learned to follow the river within and not to obstruct it with the dams of contrition and fear.

I didn't intend to stay for long. The message of Oxford was clear: move on. But before I did, I had to relive one last memory. I left the visit to Christ Church Cathedral until almost the last day. It was there that I had met Ignacio, a visiting arts professor from Madrid. We were both standing at the back listening to yet another beautiful Christmas concert that Oxford churches excel in. I had seen him before, walking down the High Street on his way to Queen's College where he was lecturing and writing. It was impossible not to notice him. He was a tall, Byronic figure with longish white-grey hair and a classically handsome face. He looked as if he had stepped from a Caspar David Friedrich painting, the last romantic or the last Spanish gentleman to walk the streets of these prosaic times. Despite his appearance, he was warm and approachable, ever willing to talk. When I heard his accent, I began to speak in Spanish, and so our friendship started. He had formed a group of Spaniards in Oxford, mostly PhD students from the colleges, who met once a week in Balliol College for lunch. They were to contribute to a book about Oxford seen through Spanish eyes. On the very night we met he invited me to join the group.

'*Eres prácticamente española, una española inglesa,*' he said with the generosity that would redeem all possible vanity about his extraordinary looks and vast culture. And being Ignacio, it was also a reference to one of Cervantes's novels: *La Española Inglesa.*

And I was, am, a Spanish English woman. I have become a strange hybrid but deeply enriched by it. I found myself enjoying our meetings in Balliol with the group of Spaniards far more than the ones with my classmates. This group was welcoming, spontaneous, joyful, creative, and accepting of me, an outsider who was also much older. Their sense of humour and their *joie de vivre* was very contagious. I discovered through them how profoundly Spain and its culture had taken root in me, and how much I had been missing the enthusiasm and warm hearts of its people.

Ignacio was a poet, a lover of art and beauty, and he also loved to help other people. All of us in that group were helped in some way or other, be it through guidance, encouragement, opportunity or just by listening to his vast knowledge of the arts. No doubt he had a shadow, but during those months he was an angel that walked in our midst. He, a Spaniard, showed me all the nooks and crannies of Oxford, invited me to join him at exhibitions and concerts, and explained all the architectural and artistic marvels of the city. He was in his early fifties, although his intense inner and outer life made him look older. But his enthusiasm and energy were like a twenty-year-old's, and he enriched all our lives with it.

The book about Oxford was eventually finished, and it was published and launched in Madrid in October of that year. There we were all reunited, Ignacio always the central figure, commanding the situation but attentive to all of us. He never missed a flick of an eyelid. The group blended in with the harsh blue sky of Madrid far better than the greyish hues of Oxford. Their olive skin no longer had a greenish tinge from the cold. They didn't stand out anymore but merged with all the other *madrileños* on the crowded streets and terraces. Here they spoke and laughed louder to keep up with the noise of the city and the deafening chatter in the bars. They greeted each other with sonorous embraces and kisses on both cheeks. They were home. Taking part in the launch of the book, drinking in the vitality of Ignacio and the students was practically the only solace in those first months of being back in Mallorca and missing the vibe of Oxford.

I worked hard at not falling in love with him. I didn't want to be another of the women who fawned around him. The difference in age, the girlfriend in Madrid and my armoured vulnerability worked well as deterrents, although he ticked every bullet point and more on my ever-lengthening list of qualities of the Right Man. Maybe the list is my protection against ever falling in love again, for I know it is impossible to find all those desired qualities in one human being. My thirty-four years of marriage with Javier scarred and scared me so deeply that I wonder how I am mentally still in one piece. But now that I have little time left, I regret not letting my guard down, of not having one last fling.

After Oxford I braced myself to return to Seaford in Sussex, the last home of my parents. I took the train down south with more unsent letters in my bag.

SEVEN

Seaford

Thursday 6 August

Dear Sam,

It's your birthday today, my second-born child. I was twenty-three and still a scared kid in many ways. You deserved a happier and more stable mother, but you were allotted one who was in survival mode most of the time, one who grew up and learned alongside you and your brother. I should have been your saviour and not you mine sixteen years ago; nor should I have allowed you to take on that role. Although perhaps it was the only way it could happen. Now you are forty-three, divorced, the father of three children and deeply scarred like your brother and me. But may you never lose your core of innocence, the pure gold of your heart that still shines through your anger and hurt. You weren't meant to live in this cut-throat world, this writhing jungle of self-interest and lies where the biggest and fattest serpents survive. For you are a *mago*, a magician. You were made to live in the world of wizards, of healers and lightworkers. Therein lies your heart. This is what sustains you while you walk along the grey concrete paths of your daily life, shut in an office while you dream of coaching burdened souls into health.

For you have vision, you see beyond the three-dimensional into what lies beyond. One day, when you are able to show the world who you truly are, when you finally confront the wolf of fear, you will rise into yourself. I hope I see it before I leave this planet. It's your time to shine.

I am staying in the White Lion, the same pub where I lodged when I came to watch Mum's ashes being scattered on the sea nearly five years ago. It's quite near the seafront, that unglamorous, empty beach with its banks of brown pebbles that match the grey sea and its swirling currents. There were never any tourists on this stark front, just the odd couple or lone walkers with their dogs, and it hasn't changed. You and Tom much preferred the other stony beach at Brighton with the gaudy attractions on the piers and the sickly smells of candy floss, fish and chips, popcorn, whelks and ice-cream along the front. I always said Brighton was a place to be sick in, and you two certainly proved it.

You would have liked the ceremony. A lifeboat from the RNLI transported Nanny's ashes and then emptied them into the sea. After that, they circled the point three times as a sign of respect. Kay and I threw some white freesias into the water and sobbed. They rode on the current for a few seconds and then were engulfed by the grey-green sea almost as quickly as the ashes were. I'm sure Nanny approved. It was what she wanted, and the sea was rough and turbulent, just as she liked it. She returned to the element she most loved. Now I want to find the plaque in memory of her and Granddad that is on one of the seats along this wind-battered front.

We were both extremely attached to her, weren't we? She grounded us with her practical, solid intelligence and her empathy. She didn't believe much in the other world, but she was willing to listen to your theories, although at times she burst the bubble with her quiet irony. How can she not be here with her sense of humour, her kindness and warmth? Surely it didn't all disappear into the sea that September morning. You still say, 'Nanny would have said this,' 'Nanny would have done that,' and I sometimes have to suppress a twinge of jealousy. Most of us are better grandparents than parents because over the years we've watched, listened and learned from innumerable mistakes. We've also become less anxious, more laid-back, and above all we have come to enjoy our grandchildren. But I must admit you would have had an easier childhood if you had lived with her in England. We know of the theory that before birth, souls choose their parents. If that is true, yours was the hardest and bravest of choices. Although maybe we have no election; maybe we travel through eternity with our soul group, suffering and learning, but most of all loving each other in all the different roles we play. You've had a tough one in this lifetime.

The journey back to Seaford is not an easy one. There are too many memories, and at times I am overwhelmed by the solitude I feel here. Because there is no one left. No one. I found out that Kay, Nanny's carer, died from a fall down the stairs a year ago. Poor woman. She must be so angry, wherever she is now! She was my only living link left with Seaford. As you know, this is a town where mostly retired people live, so not even Nanny and

Granddad's neighbours are alive. Do you remember how we used to say that Seaford and Eastbourne were the antechambers to death? *La antecámara de la muerte.* All those white heads sunning themselves along the seafront in the summer. We used to laugh then, but now I am chilled by the thought. I doubt either you or Tom will come back here, nor will Caroline. I have come to say a final farewell, to lay the ghosts of my parents to rest in this windswept little town on the East Sussex coast.

I plucked up the courage to walk past the bungalow in Lexden Road where they spent the last twenty-five years or so. I felt nothing. It is just bricks and mortar, a shell inhabited by others. There are different shrubs and flowers in the front garden and a ramp by the side door for a wheelchair, but I could still hear the children from the primary school shouting in the playing field that backed onto their garden. How Grandad used to moan about all the balls that were kicked over the fence onto his beloved flowers! I continued walking up to the countryside beyond, where you and Tom often used to go as teenagers and young men. It is still beautiful. I braced myself to tread those gnat-infested footpaths again, stopping every now and then to take deep breaths and then letting the tears roll. While you and Tom created havoc at the local tennis court, I would wander over these fields to look at the vast yellow stretches of rapeseed and to breathe the fresh, cool air. I went on these walks during so many summer holidays when I returned home to get some healing for my bruised heart and soul; and you and Tom also found respite from being cramped in a small, hot flat in the centre of Palma and from the ill humour of your father. Then I would stand and watch the sea sparkling from the top of these downs, the white cliff of Seaford Head in the distance, and I would feel a superficial balsam momentarily soothing the anxiety rumbling within.

Today when I was walking in these hills, I remembered the last walk I had the evening before I left your father. I don't know why. It was a completely different scenario, but I need to write it down, to describe it to you. It was nearly dusk, but I kept walking along the tracks where you used to go running. The cicadas were humming in the dry grass that crackled as I strode through the small fields. I had gone through the sparse wood behind our house without touching the trees or stopping to inhale the smell of wild rosemary and thyme. My legs were scratched, mosquito bites swelling into angry red lumps on my pale skin, but I felt no discomfort. Sweat was trickling down the back of my neck and I was no longer bothering to wipe the tears and snot away. I hadn't eaten that day, but hidden reserves of energy were opening somewhere in my overworked nervous system. But you were there, waiting at a friend's house, waiting to support and help me in one of the most difficult decisions of my life.

Now I am accompanied by ghosts, I hope, and I can only heal myself, as you are doing now, Sam. But the magic is gone because there is no Nanny to go back to; no one waiting for us in that modest bungalow, no one to listen to us and soothe us with advice and home-made cakes. Grandad was missed, but the death of your grand-mother left a huge hole in our hearts. But I think that hole is filled with the love she sends us from wherever she travelled to – I hope to a heaven of peaceful gardens with cherry trees under which she can sit and drink tea and listen to the birds and the radio, or to seas where she can float and be gently rocked in endless peace. She didn't need much else as she got older. I used to watch her and think she was slowly being whittled away until only her true essence remained. She became wise in her old age; an example of how we can grow and learn even up to the hour of our death.

I am grateful you had those holidays in England, that month of normality and tranquillity with your grandparents. At least with them you knew there were other ways of living that were not tinged with your father's madness or depression or manic laughter, usually at the expense of someone else's faux pas or mishaps. In England we would relax, put on weight and get some colour that was healthier than our wan tans. Returning to Mallorca was never easy, was it? And it probably wasn't easy for your father, either, who'd had weeks of doing what he wanted without having to resort to all the subterfuge and lies he based his daily life on.

You cried, and cry, in all ways except through tears. Most of all you cry through anger or in silence when you withdraw completely into yourself. And you show your exceptional inner strength when you have to deal with situations that most of us crumble beneath: when you helped me escape from the hell I was living in; when you came to tell me, a year and a half later, of your father's death. With no tears, in a flat, beaten voice, you said these six words:

'Papá is dead. He hanged himself.'

Then, after calling a friend to sit with me, you went off to deal with the police. You phoned your brother in Barcelona, the rest of the family, and took the brunt of everyone's shock and sorrow. You arranged the funeral and made sure your elder brother carried the urn. The only time I saw you shed tears was when you leant over your father's open coffin before he was cremated; not even when the three of us scattered his ashes up in the mountains, in that place where he loved to cycle, when a solitary yellow butterfly appeared – not even then did you cry. When all was done, you disappeared into yourself in your little apartment by the sea. You hardly spoke. You lived through your grief by yourself. You wanted no one.

You were truly my saviour in helping me flee to England that eleventh of June, sixteen years ago. You opened my eyes to the fact that the cup of indignities and suffering had overflowed. You planned and staged the whole operation right down to the most insignificant detail because failure was too dangerous a possibility. You were my absolute defender, but I realised years later that I should never have let you intervene. I should never have allowed you to carry that responsibility, that burden. Then when you married and later turned your back on me for a year, I understood why. You needed to reconcile yourself with your father and lift the crippling weight of guilt. And you have achieved it. You have forgiven yourself and him. You have weighed up the good against the bad. You have given him recognition, in spite of everything. Above all, you needed to accept all that he was and to love him. I asked you to forgive me too, which I know you have in that good heart of yours. Now I must forgive myself.

Te quiero,
Mamá

***

I was back in Seaford, listening to the constant screeching and wheeling of seagulls, battling the bracing wind even in August. It's a wind that strips you of all the superfluous, starting with hairstyles, shattering egos until it finally leaves you with your own solitude. That is how I felt in this unassuming little seaside town: utter loneliness. I could have made a trip into decadent Brighton, only half an hour away by train, or to the more conventional East-bourne on the other side of Seaford. But I knew I had to stay and get to the very depths of my sadness with no distraction. Brighton, where I was born and lived for the first two years of my life, held little attraction for me now that I could no longer accompany my mother there and watch her enjoy her old stomping ground. And East-bourne with its more respectable, sedate atmosphere held even less now there was no desire for shopping centres or damp sandy beaches that could never compete with Mallorca's glorious *playas*.

I didn't even bother to take a walk along the South Downs to catch a glimpse of the Seven Sisters in all their magnificence. That scenery belonged to the memory of my parents when as a yearly ritual, they would ask me to stroll with them, picking our way through yellow gorse bushes right up to the cliff edge; although the Sussex coastline still appears in dreams when I fly above the

Cuckmere Valley, the Downs, and then veer down to the sea crashing over the rocks. These are my deepest roots, the ones that only stir when my subconscious emerges in sleep. But this month I spent most of my time sitting on the uncomfortable beach, breathing in the intense ozone of the English Channel and watching the sea devoid of boats but replete with seabirds circling and swooping to catch the odd fish. How different to the lolloping summer waves of the Mediterranean that lull you into thinking that all is well, that life is easy, easy. This sea is harsh and temperamental, unwelcoming and unadorned. There are no tourists, no bathers. The currents are too dangerous and drag everything under in seconds, like my mother's white freesias. This sea and wind whip you and wake you to every crude reality till the salt stings your wounds, till you can bear no more.

Here on this beach, I unravelled to the core. I lived through my parents' deaths and wished they were there beside me so I could tell them I loved them and hold their hands as we hardly ever did in their lifetime. I wished I could have broken through their embarrassment at showing their feelings, especially my father's. I would have told him how I saw him watching with such compassion a solitary dog fox walking down the street searching for food one snowy January night; how he fought back the tears when I married Javier; that the only hug he had given me in his entire life was when I finally left my husband and fled to England. Why wait for extreme situations to show your love? There is so little time. Now you are ghosts, and I can only hug you in my imagination and in my dreams.

What else can we do to make this short time here on earth worthwhile?

And on this beach, I remembered how I had lain here sixteen years ago with a shattered heart, a heart so heavy with pain and sorrow that it was a physical weight in my chest. I had fled Mallorca in June and wasn't to return until the end of August when María Consuelo took me into her house until I could find somewhere to rent. How grateful I was and still am to her for that generosity, especially when I could see in her anguished eyes that she didn't know how to cope with my emotional state or really understand why I had left and then returned. But she tended me that first helping hand to rebuild a life without Javier.

My parents put up with me that summer but by mid-August my father, especially, was urging me to go back to Mallorca, to find somewhere to live and start again. At the time I felt a little rejected and hurt, but now I see how right he was. I could no longer live in England; my work, my friends were in Mallorca, with or without Javier. England was a refuge, but no longer my home. I had created in my mind an idealised version of the country I left at nineteen, but now there were too many aspects I could no longer relate to. Mallorca had seeped into my bones and blood drip by drip during all those years, in spite of the suffering and hardships. It had gradually become separate from Javier and his instability. It had become part of me, right down to the mosquitoes in summer and the yellow pine pollen in March; so much so that the first thing I always did when stepping out of the plane at

Palma airport was to take a deep breath and smell the pine resin and the sea. I was home. And here I would die.

Fleeing from Mallorca that summer was carefully planned by Sam in three weeks, from the twentieth of May to the eleventh of June. On the twentieth I had received a phone call at five a.m. which was supposed to be for Javier. It was from the latest of his flings, this time an illegal Algerian immigrant aged twenty-four with two small children, whom he had deceived into believing he was divorced and to whom he had been lending money. When she failed to return the money, he had threatened to denounce her to the police. Hysterical with fear, she explained everything to me in broken English and Spanish. She told me how Javier had brought her and the children to our house while I was in England for a week with my sons, celebrating my parents' fiftieth wedding anniversary. When I confronted Javier, he shrugged it off, laughing, and said it was 'all over', that she was '*solo una putita*'. My pity for his mental health finished at that moment. Never had such direct evidence been handed to me, and even as I felt the kick of shame and indignity, even as the thin walls I had built around me began to crumble, I knew a door was opening for me. My first thought while I listened to the girl sobbing on the phone was *Now I can go*.

Javier had been working nights for five years. He was supposed to be answering phone calls and checking the late-night coaches that arrived after dropping off tourists at their hotels. A lot of the time he would be drunk at a nearby table-dance club, which is where he picked up the Algerian girl. Then he would sleep through most of the day. Those final weeks, when he left for work in the evenings, I gradually packed a case with essential belongings and hid it under the bed in the spare bedroom. I had to explain the situation to the headmaster at school because Sam had bought a plane ticket for the eleventh of June and school didn't finish until the twenty-second. How can I ever forget the generosity of the principal and his team, who allowed me to give in my end-of-year marks two weeks early and let me go, more worried about my safety than the fact that I had to miss school? These Mallorcans are in my heart forever. I lived on automatic pilot those weeks and lost about five kilos. I could only think of getting away without Javier finding out. He assumed my silence and long face was from anger and jealousy and that I would get over it, as always. He never imagined the volcano about to erupt.

Sitting on the beach, listening to the drag and crackle of the sea on the stones as the current pulled backward and forward, I relived the night before I left Javier and fled from Mallorca. The details are imprinted on my brain in indelible ink.

***

I wait until he leaves for work at ten p.m. At midnight, when I am sure any snooping neighbour will be in bed, I drag the suitcase from under the bed, lock it and bump it down the stairs. I open the front door and making the least noise possible, I pull it down the steps, onto the pavement and wheel it to my car parked across the road. The light from the streetlamps pursues me as if I were an escaping convict. I drop the car keys – the metal clink resonates against me in the silence. I keep my eyes down. My shaking hands eventually open the boot, and I heave the case inside. My breath is coming out in short, shallow bursts as I return swiftly to the house. I am sweating, my heart is banging against my ribcage, and I cannot stop trembling. I don't go back to bed; I lie on the sofa fully dressed and wait for the morning. I clutch my bag to my stomach, the cat curled up beside me. I have checked my travel documents, passport and money at least ten times.

The light filtering through the shutters stirs me from my semi-doze. The bag has slipped onto the floor and the cat has found a more tranquil spot in the armchair. The dawn chorus of the eleventh of June begins, backing up my momentum. The moment of dawn is heavy with expectancy as the new day prepares to spill itself forth. The world holds its breath in the profound silence that ensues when the birds are quiet. And I am part of this expectancy. I, too, am pushed forward and out.

I get up, stiff and achy from the sofa. My head is pounding, my clothes creased, but I am no longer trembling. I open the doors that lead onto the patio and the cat, my beautiful chocolate point Siamese, slips through. He picks his way delicately through the grass which glistens darkly with dew. Then his brown back disappears behind the sombre cypress trees.

I look at the half-grown garden. It is the only thing I will miss about the terraced house we finally moved to from the cramped little flat a few years back. The hibiscus flowers are still furled, the bougainvillea still in shadow. I wonder who will tend to it now. Will it be left to overgrow to a mass of long, yellow grasses and robust flowering weeds? Or maybe someone else will nurture it, keep the soil moist so the birds can pick at the worms and the cat try to hunt them still.

And because this is a slow death, I have time to embalm the image of the garden awakening to the morning light, of the chocolate-brown cat elegantly prowling his territory, even the memory of Javier on a good day, watering the grass and singing *rancheros*. This has remained fresh and solid and unfading in my memory. This did exist.

Where does love go when a relationship ends? What remains of those feelings that sustained your very being when you surrendered heart and soul to the person who you thought you would journey with in this lifetime? Does it dry out like old rose petals that are dispersed by the wind? Or is it encapsulated in a strip of the universe that we can dip into and savour when we can no longer bear our loneliness? And we can say: this is registered for all eternity?

At seven-thirty I hear Javier's car drawing up, the door slamming. I pick up the school folders, take my bag and open the front door. We cross on the threshold. '*Buenos días*' is all that is said. He imagines I have my first class at eight. He avoids my eyes; I cannot look into his. The front door closes. It is over.

I get into my car, throw the folders on the back seat and drive slowly down the hill that leads onto the motorway. But this time I don't take the turning for Palma. I head towards the coast, to one of the tourist resorts, S'Arenal. I find a parking space easily. At this time of the

morning most of the tourists are sleeping off their hang-
overs.

I remember as if it were now, how the half-moon was
still visible, the sea lapping serenely. A solitary jogger ran
along the promenade lined with palm trees. The only
noise was from a beach tractor turning over the sand,
cleaning the rubbish from the night's revelry. I would
have stripped off my clothes bit by bit, walked over the
sand, scattering the scavenging seabirds, and waded into
the luminous sea. I would have let myself drift out and
out until I was cleansed by salt and air, until I remembered nothing.

But I locate the bar Sam has told me to wait in. It has
just opened. A waiter is pulling white plastic chairs onto
the terrace. He looks tired and bad-tempered and ignores
me. I have to wait ten minutes before he brings me a
slopped *café con leche*. But I am in no hurry. My plane takes
off at one o'clock. I have five hours to wait and think
about thirty-four years of my life married to the wrong
man and to analyse why I took so long to get away.

Sam arrives on his bike ten minutes later. He looks
tired and tense. In silence we wheel the bike to my car
and heave the case onto the back seat to make space.
Then Sam removes the wheels of the bike and squashes
the parts into the boot. They hang precariously out the
back as we slowly drive to the airport without speaking.
Sam drops me at the entrance and hauls out the suitcase.
There is a quick hug and then he is off in my car. No
looking back. When his father wakes, he will be waiting
to tell him I have left.

It is too early to check in, so I wait, immobile amidst the swirling hordes of passengers. I am just another anonymous traveller carrying my own private tragedy. Outside are the white monoliths of the airport and I feel protected by them, as if they were ancient, sacred stones which harbour all those within them. No one knows where I am, apart from Sam. I am momentarily safe.

At half past twelve my flight is announced, and I go to wait in the queue which is composed mainly of red-brown tourists going home. I wonder what kind of home I'm going back to or where home really is. The tourists' squealing cheeriness punctures my eardrums like a continual firing of arrows. I wish I could disappear, roll up like a prodded bug and hide in a dark corner. By now Javier will have woken and Sam will have told him. I can imagine the fury darkening the pupils of his blue eyes, the beast surfacing. I quell my fear and board the plane.

The plane takes off and my heart is heavy with sadness and relief, but somewhere there is a bird singing.

***

Rocked by the rhythmic swell and dip of the sea, I fell asleep thinking that a plane which soared overhead was the one that had flown me to Seaford all those years ago. As I awoke, still on the threshold of sleep and full consciousness, in the state when our subconscious speaks clearly to us and from where our clearest intuitions arise, I surrendered my sorrow, my guilt, my burden. I let it all be engulfed by that rough sea that was the burial chamber of my mother's ashes. I realised I had come back to Seaford searching for the solace only my mother could give me, but I had discovered that I could only give it to my-self when I was finally able to lay down the load. No therapy had stripped me as bare of my protective layers as those hours on Seaford beach.

And Sam. It seems he was destined to be my saviour, even at the expense of his father's suicide, even though we both paid such a high price for his courage in the following years. I could not have left without his help or his vision. I was too broken. He put the pieces together and sealed the cracks with gold paint. Then it was up to me to float or sink in new waters.

Where would I go now? I was in need of spiritual convalescence, somewhere my heart could rest awhile, where I could just be and quieten my overactive mind. Ireland. The land I wished I had been born in, the land of fairy rings and soft, welcoming wildness. Ireland.

EIGHT
Dunlewey, Ireland

Tuesday 1 September

Dear Cliona,

If I could write the epitaph for your tombstone (which I know you won't have as your ashes will be settled somewhere in Ireland, and God forbid you should die before me), it would be: SHE WAS LOVED. Because that is what you are: loved. You once told me that you would have liked to be the most special person in someone's life. I understood that so well as we are both widows of men who certainly didn't make us feel 'special' in the way we needed. But the fact is that you are branded as extremely special in the lives of nearly everyone that you have close contact with. Being with you is like being at home, where you can relax, take off your mask and be ninety per cent yourself. I say this because everyone, including you, keeps that last ten per cent in their innermost sanctum. But with you we can take off our make-up, show our scars and spots, have a rant about whatever is bothering us, and know that we will be listened to with empathy and not judged. You are a soother of souls; you nurture my soul as I think I do yours. Over the years you have become the wise old woman everyone seeks out, and you are often pulled in many directions to attend to them all. I used to feel a little jealous that I could not always have your undivided attention when I was with you, but I realised that you had taken on a role that fulfilled part of your own personal growth, that was somehow part of your destiny. You are friendly and gregarious and enjoy being part of different social groups, whereas I am more the introvert and prefer one-to-one communication. But most of all there is a joyous lightness about you, an almost stubborn refusal to see the shadow in other people and life in general; an attitude which your daughters sometimes consider an irritating positivism, but maybe this is the stuff angels are made of.

Our friendship began sixteen years ago, the same year I separated from Javier. I had just started going to yoga classes which is where I met you. You stood out, tall, auburn-haired and blue-eyed amongst the smaller *mallorquinas*, and your aura of goodness and gentleness inspired me to approach you after the first class, something my reserved self would not usually do. I asked if you were English. You proudly replied in a soft Dublin accent, 'No, I'm Irish.' Your pride in all things Irish and your profound love for Ireland is something I envy and wish I had for England. I can only remember, not feel, that love for Devon and Somerset. The landscape of the west of England has many things in common with Ireland, although not its wildness. You transmitted your love of Ireland to me, and when I was finally able to visit your island five years ago, it felt like a homecoming. I knew the landscape, rejoiced in the wild dog roses and cowslip trembling in the breeze, the trees and fences softened by twilight. I loved the countryside, ungroomed and wilder than in England, just left to do its own thing and roll out its beauty unhindered. Is it these surroundings that make the Irish so cheerful and friendly and helpful and lovers of life? I could go on and on with the adjectives. Does the solidarity and the smiling face come from overcoming so much suffering and hardship? Is it from unshakeable values that kept the spirit alive even under the dead weight of despair in the times of the political and religious Troubles? You are strong, Ireland, and you have the lyricism of the poets in your blood. I wish to be like you and keep a smile on my face, no matter what.

But in social gatherings, Cliona, when you had had a little wine and were not so careful of your words, you also transmitted a deep-rooted dislike of the English, the old enemy, who had scarred your land and people with such brutality in the past. And being so profoundly Irish, that collective aversion was sunk deep in your genes, a wound you carried in your psyche from previous generations. I sank under the shame of the English; I felt saddened and humbled by the injustice and violence of my forebears. In a state of masochistic contrition, I read up on what the English had done in Ireland and was relieved that at least a quarter of me was Polish and not English. But soon we forgot about our Irishness or semi-Englishness as our friendship grew. We both had to graft onto a foreign tree and in many ways our experience has been similar. Both our husbands were called Javier and we both struggled to make sense of our lives here, to understand why we didn't pack up and leave after the first year of being misfits in one of Franco's strongholds. You became a widow a year after me, but you at least had the clear conscience of having looked after your husband until the end. Your freedom did not come at a price.

I remember telling you in the little café near your house, in the early days of our friendship, that Javier had committed suicide. I had only had the chance to go to a couple of our yoga classes before I ran off to England, and you had come to see me once in my little rented apartment when I returned, so we didn't yet know each other in depth. The news shocked you. You swallowed hard but no words came. You kept your eyes down on the cheap plastic table we were sitting at and slowly let the news sink in. And even then, you said very little. What was there to be said? Your Javier was dying of cancer at the time, and you were deep in the process of caring for a man who had given you little or no love, but who at least had not hounded you all the days of your married life. And as we whispered to each other's souls in those stark days of suffering and transformation, we understood more clearly our mistaken roles as wives of unhappy Mallorcan men, hemmed in by ancient prejudice and broken by traumatic childhoods, who should have married into their own people. You understood my conflicting emotions: my guilt and relief; my desolation on knowing how lonely Javier was, how he would ask my sister-in-law to hold his hand when she went to visit him, how he had begged Sam to live with him, how he had realised one snowy day in February that he had no future, nothing to live for, how the scribbled note he left broke our hearts. *I'm sorry. You three have been the best part of my life.* And yet I knew I had the opportunity to rebuild a different life with time. It took at least a decade. Failing health and a heart condition were the result of my feelings of guilt and sorrow. It has only been in the last four or five years that I can think of this with any objectivity and talk to you less and less about it.

We have watched each other grow into independent women, both of us half wishing for an idealised new partner but at the same time fearful of losing that prized independence that came in our fifties. We ventured into the field of alternative healing, of reiki and other less known techniques; you into voluntary hospice work, me into writing. Grandchildren were born, young old age began. We started to like ourselves again, to make up for lost time by doing courses, going on little trips to the other Balearic Islands and the mainland, being so busy we were often exhausted. Even now there is a sense of urgency to discover, to learn, to recover what was held back during those years of spiritual and emotional hunger, of scarcity on all levels and in all hues. It was like trying to walk in shoes that were the wrong size. Every step taken was crippling but we carried on, always hopeful that one day we would be given the right ones. It was only after leaving Javier that I realised only I could kick them off and get myself a new pair.

So here I am, back in Donegal and staying with Nerea. This time I'm not in Sligo but in Dunlewey, in a little cottage from where I can see Mount Errigal. I open the curtains every morning and there it is, majestic, mysterious and ancient as this land which welcomes me again. I am so grateful to Nerea, my Mallorcan-Irish friend who has finally succumbed to the pull of Ireland and come to live here, at least until she is pulled in the opposite direction by Mallorca. She is another of my dear Mallorcan friends from school whose generosity and warm heart have found a large space in my own. Our hearts are always expanding to make room for more beloved beings that come into our lives, don't you think? As you know, she is Sam's age and could be my daughter, but age is no impediment for true friendship. She goes off to work, teaching Spanish at a nearby school, despairs daily of her pupils, and I can wander and do my own thing. But in her free time, she takes me off on road and walking trips. I am feeling healthier by the minute in this unpolluted air from the fresh winds off the Atlantic coast. My old wounds are being soothed and sometimes I only feel like sleeping. In fact, I have just woken up from a long siesta and for a moment I couldn't figure out where I was! While I am waiting for Nerea to come and pick me up for another Irish music evening at the pub, I have been thinking of the time I stayed with you at your daughter's house in Kildare and the walks we went on. The one that most comes to mind was the long trek we did along the Grand Canal that links Dublin to Galway. You strode ahead as always, my tough Irish friend, and I panted behind, stopping every now and then to get my breath back. I remember seeing a silver-blue heron rising from the grasses along the banks of the canal. You always said I reminded you of a little bird. I wasn't quite sure I liked that image of nervous vulnerability, but now I would like to be that heron in its dance of majestic freedom. Kildare was damp, mild and lush, and reminded me again of

Devon in its soft greenness. The wildness and the light of the north-west coast awakened another part of me.

From Kildare you took me for a quick trip into Dublin for my first encounter with the city. The centre was smaller than I had imagined, without the hard hustle and bustle of cities like London. Nigh on impossible to feel lost and lonely in Dublin. I liked the stone, darkened by constant rain on the buildings, and didn't it rain that day! You took me for a ride on one of those sightseeing buses and the heavens opened as soon as we boarded. The rain lashed so heavily down the windows that I could only just glimpse where it was taking us. I remember a huge expanse of parkland, Phoenix Park, where you said the president of Ireland has his official abode. I remember the Liffey River, the Guinness Brewery, Kilmainham jail and Halfpenny Bridge seen through a veil of water. All to be seen again one day in fair weather. I also remember we were the only ones on the bus, shivering in our raincoats, our noses pressed to the front window trying to decipher where we were going. We later took shelter in Bewley's, that beautiful art lovers' café, and as we devoured our scones, you seemed so much a part of Dublin that I wondered what you had been doing in Mallorca all these years. Because you have retained your Irishness more than I have my Englishness. I am a hybrid, but you are ninety-five per cent Irish still.

I am more tired than I realised from my travels, yet at the same time I have never been more awake. My seventy years are catching up on me and I don't know if I will make the whole year as I planned. Maybe I need to rest, with one eye open, like migrating birds on the wing. And money is also running short. But I don't mind. I am quite at peace with myself. You might well see me by Christmas, my friend. *Anam cara.*

Love you,
Elspeth

***

This was the second time that I had stayed with Nerea. Five years ago, I had taken a short break from my course in Oxford and spent three days in Sligo where she was living with her boyfriend. Three glorious days of March sunshine to enhance my first visit to Ireland and let it seep into my blood. And it was a Mallorcan girl, the same age as Sam, who generously took me to the places she knew I would love. The first was a walk through Hazelwood Forest where we sat in front of the lake and imagined Yeats there getting inspiration for the poems that moved us both so much; then the visit to Drumcliffe to see his tomb. We imagined setting up poetry recitals back in Mallorca to honour the great poet. We haven't done it so far, but there is still time. And so many more trips were packed into those three days: gazing at Benbulben mountain and Lough Gill as Nerea and I drove slowly by in her old Seat; walking through the little streets of Sligo and stopping at pubs where there were always singers and musicians well filled with Guinness or whiskey. Out in the country I needed to touch the grass, run my fingers along the stone walls, so as not to forget any detail of those days nor how we were chased by a flock of sheep in the field behind her house. They thought we were new *pastoras,* shepherdesses, bringing them their feed; how we laughed

115

and screamed, like two little kids enjoying the fright and the run to safety.

And here I was again in another, more rural part of north-west Ireland with my dear friend Nerea. She is another evolved Mallorcan in her forties who has merged the best of Balearic traditions with contemporary times; she has managed to temper the negative aspects of soulless modernity with the kinder values of Mallorcan customs. These new Mallorcans are respectful and deeply loyal to family; they still pay visits to their old grandma and eat and argue together on Sundays. Most of them still think Mallorca is the best place in the world, but they are eager to travel and to learn without the sexual and religious prejudice of the previous generations. They are no longer the islanders who look with suspicion on any newcomer, a *foraster*, who could never be one of them. These younger generations want to mix, they want to learn and integrate the new. They are curious, forceful and passionate one minute, then fall back into states of extreme relaxation which even the most laid-back *payés*, Mallorcan countryman, idling on a Sunday afternoon, couldn't equal. Theirs is a freedom I wish could have been mine at their age. Then *la Isla de la Calma* would also have been my paradise.

Nerea: hospitable, enthusiastic, curious, affectionate, impatient, hot-blooded and short-tempered; sweet and clever, seductive and shrewd, adventurous and responsible, sentimental and practical. She is the New Mallorcan, another good friend I made in my last years at school. She is small and shapely with dark hair and large brown eyes. She is the stereotype of what many Anglo Saxons and

Celts would call a typical Spanish beauty. In a sense, she is a more evolved version of Marisol. But she doesn't dye her hair blonde, and those huge eyes are sincere. They are not the staring, unblinking ones of Marisol, always on guard, neither are they the anguished, darting ones of María Consuelo. In thirty years, Mallorca has been transformed.

Nerea is a free spirit living in Ireland but carrying Mallorca in the deepest recesses of her heart. The Irish character goes well with the Mallorcan one. They are both island people, fun-loving, sentimental and warm-hearted; they are spontaneous, relaxed and able to live the moment. Their culture is alive and vibrant, part of their daily lives. Poetry and music lie deep, especially in the Irish soul, and the pubs are often like mini concert halls. Gaelic predominates in this north-western corner of Ireland but not so much in the rest of the country. The Mallorcan language is many steps ahead in that respect. They have both been invaded countless times, but any bitterness now lies mostly with past generations. Their approach is: the sun is shining, get out and enjoy it. I have money to-day, let's go out for a meal. You're in a bad humour? I'll leave you be till it passes.

And Nerea let me be. She let me sleep off my tiredness and be nurtured. We ate when we felt like it or wanted to cook in her chaotic kitchen, a mix of Irish and Mallorcan bric-a-brac. She would often say in her Mallorcan-Irish accent: 'I think I'm starving you, you're so thin and pale', and then rush about clanging pots and pans in an effort to concoct some kind of a meal. But we would sometimes snack in the various pubs and cafés we stopped in on our road trips along the Atlantic coast. The light in that part of Ireland is indescribable. It's not the white summer brightness of Mallorca, but I was struck by the luminosity of the pale sky, a huge open sky that makes you feel unshackled and want to run along wild beaches even at my age. It was a little gift from the gods not to have arrived in bad weather. We watched the sun setting in pink and purple from the dunes of those unpolluted beaches, the clean wind whipping colour into our cheeks. Another day we saw the mist rising over the Derryveagh Mountains as we sat in the car eating crisps and drinking flask coffee. Heaven. There is a grace in this unspoilt corner of Ireland. You can feel it still in the abandoned thatched cottages and in the ruins of roofless Dunlewey church, stark and lonely in what is left of its darkened white marble and blue quartzite walls. It overlooks the Poisoned Glen, an area brimming with legend that was impossible to disbelieve when you looked at the shimmering lakes down in the valley below and the sombre mountains surrounding it all, like guardians of ancient secrets. Standing inside the roofless church, I felt I was in a sanctuary where only the initiated could step. I made a silent apology and stepped outside.

On the same day Nerea took me to another kind of sanctuary, to the grounds of the local white witch's house. She had been killed in a car accident the previous year and was already shrouded in myth. It was tucked away, as you would expect any witch's cottage to be, in woodland thick with briars and dripping leaves. The little house was locked up and we walked around the ramshackle gardens, whispering and slightly on edge. We were probably trespassing on a little haven dotted with magic symbols, but curiosity got the better of us. In one of the clearings was a fairy ring, complete with a hawthorn tree in the centre. How could you not believe in fairies in this part of Ireland where everything seems to coax them to settle and where they and their legends are treated with the utmost respect? No one dares to step inside a fairy ring if they don't want major misfortune to befall them. Yet only the fairy ring, the grass and trees, would eventually survive. The house already had a run-down, melancholy air about it. Unless someone else took it on, its fate would be like the ruins of Dunlewey church and the abandoned thatched cottages I saw on my walks. Death and decay are constantly around us; only the hills, the lakes and the mountains remain. But I suspect the secrets buried under the church and in the witch's house must remain in some parallel world we tap into when we sense their presence, as I did, with a weird buzz ringing in my ears, the hairs rising on my body like warning sensors. As my body weakens, my sixth sense grows stronger. As the layers crumble away, the veils of the other world become more transparent. Death no longer is a menacing figure but a beckoning finger into another wiser world.

After my stay in Ireland, I hardly recognise my twenty, thirty, forty, fifty, even sixty-year-old selves, but they are there somewhere in my psyche. What I identify with is the self I am now, a self that knows how to be alone and even enjoys it at times. Because even in solitude I have my tribe of beloveds that flow and contract around me like the currents of this sea, sometimes scattered by strong winds when some of you must move on to new horizons but always dancing in my dreams at night.

Ireland opened my heart. I felt it expand and lighten in the peace of this wild nature. My rational, overthinking mind was on hold. I had connected to my childhood self in Devon and to the purity of a child's unfiltered vision. Here in Ireland the power and peace of nature transformed me. There was nothing between me and these hills, nothing to pollute this beauty. I sometimes forgot who I was or simply didn't care. In the end we are all swept away and become part of this indifferent magnificence.

The need to go home was stirring within me, but I couldn't yet go back to Mallorca. I decided the return journey would include a detour to mainland Spain. Madrid or Barcelona? Madrid. Barcelona had too much in common with Mallorca, was too close in culture and proximity. Madrid was the heart of Spain; it smelt different, the air was harder, and in some respects, it felt like a different country.

NINE
Madrid

Friday 2 October

Dear María del Mar,

In my slow meander back to Mallorca I decided to stop in Madrid, this heart of Spain full of grandeur and pride. Strangely enough, or maybe not so, I think of you, my oldest Mallorcan friend, while I walk these streets teeming with people and frenetic activity as if the world were going to end tomorrow. I imagine you as a young Classics student fresh from Mallorca, one of the very few that came to study at a university in Madrid over fifty years ago. And there is something in your character which connects to the proud showiness of the *madrileños*, an uninhibited lust for life, a directness which is at the other end of the spectrum to the slow, suspicious reserve of the older generation of Mallorcans. I can see you thirsting for the stimulus of this witty, quick-thinking people; for the art galleries, museums, theatres, flea markets, and endless cafés and tapas bars, always full of noisy, laughing clients. The *madrileños* know how to live with intensity and passion. That is how I would describe you: intense and passionate. Madrid fitted you well, María del Mar. It left its mark, even in your upright bearing and the roguish twinkle in your brown eyes, and in your rich *castellano*, which isn't contaminated with Mallorcan infiltrations and pronunciation. You're the only Mallorcan I know who can give a good rendering of a *chotis madrileño*, the traditional dance of Madrid. And unlike the majority of Mallorcans, to you Madrid is a thousand times superior to Barcelona.

We have been friends for over forty years, although it wasn't easy to become your friend initially. You used to look at me askance during my first year at the school as if you were thinking *What is this foreign intruder doing here?* as you walked by with your bunch of ultra-Mallorcan buddies. At first, I was a little cowed by this older teacher of Latin and Greek who walked around as if she owned the place. But there was something about your outspoken irony and near hysterical outbursts that made me want to get to know you. You were totally thrown when I walked up to you in the bar one day in our frenetic twenty-minute break where everyone was pushing to grab a quick coffee and sandwich. I simply said: 'Have I done anything to offend you?' I knew I hadn't, but I had to break through your wall of prejudice somehow. After all, you are nearly ten years older than me and in those days a foreigner or a *forastera* was immediately placed under suspicion. Little did you imagine that I was to become one of your closest friends, even more so than your Mallorcan ones. When I said those words, you momentarily lost your guard and I glimpsed a tender vulnerability, even a shyness, which endeared me to you there and then. You quickly recovered and answered: '*¡Por supuesto que no!* Whatever made you think that?' From then on, our friendship grew, gradually but steadily, as I adapted and put down roots in Mallorcan soil.

You have been my official guide to Mallorca, María del Mar. You took me out and showed me the precious seascapes and terraced landscapes, the hidden beauty spots, the sanctuaries tucked into sacred mountains, and quiet villages in the central plains of red earth and low stone walls. I came to love this land through you on our many excursions, where you proudly told me the names of plants, shrubs and trees with the knowledge of an expert botanist. And through you I also came to understand in depth the old Mallorcan character, its profound connection with sea and earth and its need to protect this once paradise that is now slipping into speculators' hands. Your generous, passionate spirit revealed the wonder of this Mediterranean island to me and prevented me from languishing in my unhappiness. And I could lend an empathetic ear to your own.

I remember my first visit to your house on the outskirts of Palma, the backdrop of hills extending to the horizon. The countryside was still green from the spring rains and dotted with almond and olive trees gnarled and stunted from decades of implacable heat. It was early June, and every flowering shrub, tree and climber was vibrant with blossom. The fragrance of jasmine, honeysuckle and wild rose mingled in the soft air. You had laid out supper on your patio which led down to a garden overgrown with chamomile, lavender, rosemary and marjoram, all struggling for space. They trailed over large earthenware pots of oregano, thyme and basil. 'I occasionally cut it back, but mostly it does what it wants,' you said. You had prepared *tumbet*, one of my favourite Mallorcan dishes: layers of fried potato, courgette, aubergine and red peppers covered in home-made tomato sauce and seasoned with garlic and bay leaves. We mopped up the sauce with chunky slices of coarse brown bread and relaxed back in our chairs with a glass of wine. The evening wore away like old velvet to a background of cicadas and the intense perfume of *galán de noche*, a night jasmine. What a gift! The first of many you have given me over nearly forty years. Replete with good food and wine, we talked way into the night and began to understand each other's sufferings and look over cultural barriers into what lay beyond. We travelled far into understanding each other's territory so that now, being Mallorcan or *Inglesa* has little or no significance at all in our friendship.

Half of you is pure Mallorcan, like the little village where you were born, deep in the heart of the island, and sometimes you like to play at being the *madona*, the strong Mallorcan woman who rules the household, steeped in ancient customs and folklore. I've noticed that this side of you usually arises when you are in the company of fellow Mallorcans and you become the quintessence of *mallorquinidad*. It's almost as if you were acting a part in a local play and, I have to admit, it amuses me no end. Because there is another part of you that is wild, rebellious and frustrated, like a bridled thoroughbred. If you had been a man, you would have been an explorer of dangerous unknown territories, a mine deactivator or part of an expedition to climb Everest where you would have proudly planted the Mallorcan flag. As a woman of your generation, you never really succumbed to the suffocating limits of your culture, although you certainly paid lip service to it. An only child, you were kept in, married to free yourself and then fell into another cage of your own making. Even though the door was open, you were unable to leave. You supported me when I left Javier, but you would never have separated from your own husband and were deeply shocked when I finally left mine. Husbands could be eternally moaned about, cried over, even despised, but the excruciating pain of a bad marriage was to be endured until death do us part. Now you and your husband are both in your eighties and can hardly be in the same room together. You were born two decades too early for your passionate temperament, María del Mar, and I see you constantly swallow the bile of your anger and frustration.

You give the love you have been denied in your marriage to your friends. You bestow on us the gifts of your artistic temperament. You sing, you dance, you recite poetry, you take us to see spectacular sunsets, the marvels of your garden, and then you return to the silence and loneliness of your house. Even your children have been tainted, although you have tried your best to wash away the stains and you shower them and your grandchildren with unhinged love.

Your inability to free yourself from this tragic conditioning used to sadden and anger me. But I have come to understand how after years of cultural brainwashing, it has become part of your DNA, and maybe you were too scared to undergo the emotional and mental upheaval of breaking patterns and lifelong habits. Perhaps you feel they are part of your identity. And freedom can be terrifying. I wish you peace in your big, turbulent heart and thank you for the gift of yourself and the secret Mallorca.

I salute you, queen of Mallorca!

Te quiero,

Elspeth

***

As the plane descended over the barren Meseta towards the outskirts of Madrid, I felt a twinge of regret that I was not glimpsing the Tramuntana mountain range on Mallorca's north-west coast, nor the abandoned windmills on the plains. How alien the landscape of central Spain appeared to me, how dry and void of life and beauty. Had I made a mistake? What would I do by myself in this metropolis where the air was hard and rarefied, where I couldn't smell the sea or the pine-tree resin or hear the seabirds squawking? But I had made a reservation in a *pensión*, a little hostel in Calle de Santa Isabel, the only area I knew well in Madrid. I had stayed there four years ago when Ignacio had gathered the group from Oxford for the presentation of our book. I knew I would not see him. He was away in Italy on another of his teaching trips, and in a way I was glad. I had moved on. I also needed to wander at my own pace and not go on an intense cultural tour as Ignacio would have given me.

I sniffed the cutting, drying air of this high-altitude city as I struggled out of the Metro station at Antón Martín with my bulging suitcase, just like I had four years ago. Then, I had been nervous and overexcited as I searched for Ignacio´s flat where he had invited me to stay. Now I was to look for the hostel in the same street. It was reassuring to be in a street I knew in this vast city. How different to my fearless young self when I would have taken anything that was cheap, even if it was in the most sinister *barrio* full of pimps and pickpockets, as I did once on a trip to Barcelona a year before I met Javier, before my exploring of the world was truncated.

Hostal Santa Isabel was clean and close to a market, El Prado and El Parque del Retiro. What more could I ask for? My dwindling funds meant I would be having large breakfasts in the hostel and living on tapas and *bocadillos* the rest of the day. I was in the heart of the city, surrounded by grand plazas, *teatros* and markets, and narrow, welcoming streets full of bars. Nearby was La Plaza de Santa Ana, where we had our book launch. El Ateneo de Madrid and El Museo de Arte de la Reina Sofía were just down the road. I was in *el barrio de las letras*, the literary and art quarter, where Ignacio was in his element. This was his Madrid, the one I had seen through his eyes and his enthusiasm. Now I would taste it by myself in small meandering doses, at my own pace, as a quiet observer.

I had a small balcony to my room which overlooked the narrow street with its big rubbish containers, noisy bars and buildings opposite with other *balcones* and nosy inhabitants. The first time I looked out, I imagined María del Mar walking these streets in her student years. She would have worn pencil skirts that showed off her prominent backside and pale, shapely legs. Her chestnut hair would be tied back with a colourful scarf, her white skin accentuated by a slick of red lipstick, her slightly bulging brown eyes scanning all her retina could retain. She would have talked and laughed loudly with her companions, so full of energy and life, of potential, of future. Now she is eighty, hoary and gnarled like the olive trees of her land. She no longer weeps for lost opportunity; she weeps only for loss of love, like most of us do if we reach old age. She knows that the only thing that truly heals is unconditional love.

As I looked at the man-made landscape before me, I thought of the last time I saw María del Mar. It was at the beginning of March, shortly before I left on my travels. She had invited me to her little country house high up in the hills of Puigpunyent. The house had belonged to her parents and was in need of repair, but it was built on the side of a hill and offered one of the most beautiful views of Mallorca. I sat on the terrace bordered with lavender bushes and watched her pick the last of the season's tangerines and oranges which she would oblige me to take home along with armfuls of rosemary and oregano. Nimble as a mountain goat, her white hair knotted at the nape of her neck, she scrambled up and down the slopes and inspected the other fruit trees that were soon to flower: cherry, apple, pomegranate, pear, kumquat, fig, loquat … How she nurtured and cared for it all and how she loved to share it with others. I watched the wind ruffle the silver backs of the olive trees way down in the valley. They moved in unison in great iridescent waves at the feet of the mountains that rose up behind them. The air was alive with the sound of flirting birds, of spring awakening. This Mallorca, these snippets of paradise, I carry with me wherever I go. What could I give back to María del Mar? I tried to give her what she most needed: to be listened to without judgement, and to be allowed to show and boast of her one true love, this island.

Later we sat in the old kitchen eating *pan amb oli*, bread and olive oil with cheese and serrano ham, which she always kept the larder well stocked with. I was tempted to tell her of my plan to travel for maybe a year, of my failing health, and I felt guilty for not confiding in her, as I did with my other close friends. She, they, would have understood, but telling them would have smeared the absolute freedom of my decision and actions. Their opinions or their concern for my safety and health might have rung in my ears and made me dither. This was especially true of my sons and sister. María del Mar's letter would be the last one to be sent. The ones to Marisol and María Consuelo remained in my bag. María del Mar would relish receiving an old-fashioned letter and perhaps forgive me for taking so long. She is the old Mallorca and as I get physically nearer the island, her presence looms large here in Madrid.

I felt more at ease than I thought in this great city with its elegant boulevards and well-cared-for parks. The monuments are imposing but at the same time the atmosphere is welcoming and friendly. There are many little streets to get lost in, many with private art exhibitions, bookshops and cafés. I tried to remember the places Ignacio took me to, but I only got to the Círculo de Bellas Artes. I did find El Rastro one Saturday, but the jostling crowds intimidated me and then I wished Ignacio were with me, guiding me along in his elegant clothes and enjoying admiring looks from many women and quite a few men. I forced myself to go to El Prado one rainy day, but the big museums tired me, so I contemplated a few Goya and Velázquez paintings and was then out looking for a *choco-latería,* to have some hot chocolate and churros. I seemed to need chocolate more than art some days. I also needed the living art of nature, so I spent a lot of time in El Parque del Retiro just observing and walking. Even though it was October, it felt like summer, the trees still dressed in green under the fulgent sunlight. I had my fill of the great monuments, the palaces, the Plaza Mayor, the museums. I would have gone to the theatre, but money was getting short and watching people in the park was good entertainment as I sat eating sandwiches under the canopy of the magnificent trees. Nightfall hardly muffles the noise of Madrid, but if you are close enough and listen carefully, you can hear the murmur of the trees swaying and creaking in El Retiro.

El Retiro is huge, big enough for people to run, skate and even cycle. I could have spent weeks here and not seen all it offers. I watched families rowing boats on El Estanque Grande, the big pond, how they noisily enjoyed themselves in this green lung of the city. Most Spaniards are incapable of doing anything quietly and I could hear their conversations from a distance. I couldn't help but compare the vigorous blast, the staccato, of the Spanish spoken here, with its clear-cut vowels and sharp endings, to the drawn-out, more neutral tones of a Mallorcan speaking *castellano,* as if their mouths were full of mushy potato. The Mallorcan language is slower, more patient and melodic, and inevitably infuses mainland Spanish with its own music. The *madrileños* speak and look at you directly, no beating about the bush, no standing on ceremony. Let's get on with life, don't waste time, keep moving with quick-fire blasts of energy – that is the symphony of Madrid and its inhabitants. Stimulating, radical, passionate and vital. No one sleeps much in this city so far in so many ways from *la Isla de la Calma*.

Three things left a deep impression on me in El Retiro. The first was the sight of the oldest tree in Madrid, El Ahuehuete, a Mexican conifer known as *El Abuelo,* the grandfather. I contemplated this twenty-five-metre-tall tree supposedly dating from 1633 and imagined how much Spanish history it had seen in its magnificent indifference; how many bombs had dropped nearby in the civil war, how many killed in the uprising against the French, in the famous *segundo de mayo* in 1808. They are brave, these Spaniards, strong and wilful. *Sangre y arena,* blood and sand; the name fits them well.

The second was the blackened bronze statue of the fallen angel, *El Ángel Caído,* Lucifer himself, twisted and anguished, his mouth open in terror and hatred, a serpent entwined around his legs. Who but the Spanish could think of placing such a horrific and fascinating statue in a recreation park, standing in its own fountain? Maybe it was a reminder in more religious times of how we should beware of falling from grace. It is said to be at a height of six hundred and sixty-six metres from sea level and has attracted many Satanists who consider it to be a portal to hell. I did not linger there for long.

The third was El Bosque de los Recuerdos, which is a funerary monument built on an artificial hill in the form of one hundred and ninety-two trees, dedicated to the victims killed in the terrorist attack in Madrid on the eleventh of March 2004. The silence there was profound among the hundred and seventy solemn cypress trees and twenty-two sturdy olive trees, a reminder of our fragile existence. We can snap like the twigs on these trees, like those poor commuters did just as their trains arrived in Madrid. The memorial is beautiful. At least the trees that represent the dead will continue to grow, at least they will be remembered for some generations. A huge price to pay for being a reminder of some human beings' barbarity.

I was glad to be in Madrid and to be by myself, without the overwhelming company of Ignacio. I felt, at times, as I had done those first years in Mallorca, that I had been extracted from one life and put into another, and that what had been important or a guiding reference in one became nothing in the other. Back then I had wondered who I was, but I know now where I come from and where I want to be. I'm at peace with the past, which in the great scheme of things is of such insignificance. I know, too, that to be able to reach home, you have to go away from it first. That was where I was going now: home. Mallorca. I was not going directly back to my apartment, nor was I going to tell anyone yet. I booked myself into a hostel facing the mountainside in Deià. I had one more letter to write, another one that would also not be posted.

TEN

Mallorca

I step off the plane and sniff the air. That smell again, a mixture of pine trees, resin and burnt wood that is curiously sweet. It only smells like this here. I would know where I was blindfold. I walk down the stairway, gripping the handrail. The pain in my back, my fatigue, does not hinder a resurgence of joy which rises up from the base of my spine like liquid gold. It opens the way to each vertebra, each nerve, giving new life to my blood, numbed from sitting and sheer exhaustion.

When I reach *Control de Pasaportes* it is already four in the afternoon and the heat of the beginning of November is building up. It must be at least twenty-eight degrees. The autumn rains have been scarce so far, so the free newspaper has informed me on the plane. Global warming has truly set in. Sitting in their cubicles are the two young agents of *la policía nacional,* tanned and handsome in their dark-blue uniforms. They lazily flip through my passport and beckon to the next person with the usual tired gesture. Their offhand indolence, the look of disregard which they cast upon the mass of tourists, is comforting. No hypocritical attempts at courtesy, no 'Good day, have a nice stay'. I am back.

And then, outside, the light! I had almost forgotten the unique luminosity of the island, even in November. It bounces off the white buildings and stings my unprotected eyes and mercilessly reveals my seventy-year-old skin. I rapidly take refuge in the shade and wait in the taxi queue with my two scraped suitcases. I am trembling with tiredness and nerves. I long to go to my home but I know it is not the right moment. My journey hasn't finished yet.

Once I am settled in the taxi, I let the driver fill in all the gaps of island gossip, most of it about the disastrous local politicians, about how much money the tourists brought in, and *'este puto calor'*, the 'bloody never-ending heat'. I sit back, listen, laugh and look. On comes the protective armour against dismay. It is not even nine months since I left, but the new motorway is finished, running alongside the old road where sheep graze in what is left of the fields. New buildings are sprouting, hemming in the ancient windmills. Caroline and I used to call Mallorca 'the land of a thousand potholes' fifty years back. Now it is criss-crossed by sleek motorways heavy with traffic.

When the taxi is well away from the airport I relax. There is the countryside, still brown in patches from the implacable heat; the small fields are no longer dotted with white daisies and yellow celandine as they were last March, but I can see the almond and olive trees, knotted and stunted from years of harsh sun. They are close at hand, tangible and reassuring. I breath in the fragrance of the earth through the open window. It smells of easy living, of sea and land just a step away. It smells of coming home.

The taxi begins to struggle up narrow mountain roads and the scenery changes from comforting to spectacular. It is still there: the humming silence of windswept rocks, the wind whispering through swaying trees that no speculator, no prying builder can destroy. And then the village appears. It spreads up from the valley and twists through the hillsides. It is protected by mountains, now greyish black, now splashed green and blue. They rise eternally impassive, guardians of a privileged land ejected from the sea. I feel my heart opening to the beauty. Why did I take so long to come back?

'*¡Aquí estamos señora!*' says the taxi driver. He parks in front of the hostel that is nearly at the top of a narrow, winding track, an old Mallorcan house that the owner has converted into a modest hostel. At least he did not succumb to the sumptuous sums of money offered by rich invading foreigners when he inherited this little jewel embedded in a hillside of Deià.

'*Qué tal señora, ¿cómo está?*' I am greeted by Don Antoni, a small, bald, nut-brown man in his sixties, who remembers me from previous visits with Cliona. He tries not to look shocked by my appearance, my gaunt face and hollow eyes but doesn't succeed. He rapidly tells me I am lucky to have a room as the hostel will soon be closing until the next season in March. It is small and has retained all its Mallorcan features. I can't wait to sit out on the terrace and drink in the superb view while I imagine eating a full Mallorcan breakfast of *pa amb oli* with tomato and cheese, followed by *ensaimadas*, sweet pastries. Breakfasts in Madrid were dry and tasteless in comparison to this feast. I have lost weight and sometimes I try to forget

that however much I try to eat and the nausea that sometimes plagues me, I will never recover those kilos.

'We've put you in the room you like,' he says, and I
have to restrain the urge to hug him and plant two kisses
on his white beard, although he probably wouldn't have
minded. He takes my suitcases and asks me why I have
brought so much luggage this time. I laugh at his curiosity.

'I'll tell you later, Don Antoni. *Es una historia larga.*'

He opens the shutters and lets the light flood the solid
white walls of the room. It is sparsely furnished with an
antique double bed that had belonged to Don Antoni's
grandparents. Spread over it is a hand-crocheted white
cover that is almost severe in its neatness. Were it not for
the vase of yellow chrysanthemums on the polished chest
of drawers, it could be a monk's cell – except that monks'
cells do not have expensive antique furniture. It is the
peace, the tranquillity that pervades the room which
soothes the weary traveller in body and spirit and trans-
ports them back to times when there were no mobile
phones to overheat overactive brains.

The room has the best view of the mountains and part
of the village of Deià in the valley. Way below I can see
some of the houses wreathed in vines. It is the first of
November, All Saint's Day, a national holiday, and the
village is quiet. Many villagers will have taken flowers to
the graves of their loved ones, up to the little church
where Robert Graves is buried. It is a beautiful Catholic
tradition to pile flowers on your ancestors' tombs in a
collective homage to the dead one day a year. I have no
graves to honour with flowers and at this moment, as I

lie on the bed listening to distant dogs barking and a solitary bird singing on the windowsill, I wish I did.

I wake up the next morning with one idea in my head. I will go to Orient to the field where Javier's ashes were scattered, to his grave. There I will have the conversation, albeit one-sided, that I should have had with him before he died. I can take no peonies, no roses, only a few wildflowers I might find along the way or maybe some purple and red bougainvillea leaves from Don Antoni's terrace. I will spend the morning mentally composing the last letter to the person for whom I left my own country, for whom I made this island my home. Useless now to think what would have become of us if we had never met. But I would probably have stayed on at university, been a lecturer in English. I liked the academic world, the protected bubble of study. I like to think I would have travelled widely, casting off boyfriends along the way like my deceased friend Annette. She at least fulfilled the dreams we had planned together. She lived her fifty-six years intensely before she died of breast cancer. And Javier? Maybe he would have married a Mallorcan girl who would have kept in line with the traditions, been a good housewife and good in bed, and pretended not to notice his infidelities as long as he brought money in. How can anyone understand our incongruous relationship if not from some higher karmic law? And maybe forgiveness and love are the only ways to settle karmic accounts.

I spend the morning thinking about the letter I will write to Javier and then answer emails and WhatsApp's from family and friends. When I am back home, I will put the bundle of unsent letters in a drawer where I keep my papers. Whoever finds them can decide what to do with them. Soon I will tell them all that I have returned. I will sit them down and tell them about my illness and the time I have left. And soon I will need to be admitted to hospital for treatment. But not yet. Only María Consuelo has not acknowledged my WhatsApp's, although she never has learned to use a computer or smartphone. Marisol has proudly sent me photos of her paintings; my sons, short but tender messages; Alberto and María del Mar, photos of all the beautiful things that take their fancy; and Caroline, a wistful email that is underscored with loneliness and hurt. Maybe in the end the letters I thought I would send and then didn't send were letters I had written just as much to myself as to them; to reveal to myself and understand what I wouldn't have had the courage to admit otherwise. But maybe, too, we are all bound together in a strange chain of destiny. We lean and bounce on and off each other until our journey on this planet ends. Maybe we should be more grateful for what we have learned from one another and for soothing and softening the burden of the loneliness in the core of our hearts. Maybe we should be less critical of ourselves, let go and make this last dance as sweet and light as we can. Because now that I am being stripped of what I thought was me, I know that all that matters is the love I carry in my heart and that is all that will remain of me.

The poem of my life, which will soon be ending, is created from small things, even the ordinary, in the quiet moments, not the drama or tragedy. It's in the conversation with a friend, sometimes in the effort to keep a friendship afloat; it's in the morning light slanting off the

sycamore in front of my window, even though the hooting of traffic deafens the birdsong. It's feeling truly loved,
although the moment was fleeting. It's opening my heart
to the ones I love too. It's having the gift of extreme sensitivity and seeing it passed on to my sons. It's picking up
every sound and resonating with someone's voice or a
piece of music and being deeply moved by the way words
bond together to make a line of poetry. It's knowing what
someone is feeling by the expression on their face, sens-
ing their anger, joy, sorrow, envy, sincerity or hypocrisy.
It's capturing beauty and ugliness and feeling them to the
quick. It's hurting so badly from falsehood, indifference
and lack of soul but thriving on love and generosity. As
do we all. It's knowing that love, a little pain and regret
are impregnated in the walls where we live and in the
hearts of those that remain when we are gone. In the end
I can only give thanks for so many gifts: to my parents
for giving me life and keeping me alive; to my beloved
family and friends. We are all imperfectly perfect. And
most importantly, I am grateful to you all for putting up
with me and helping me to live.

I have no car and there is no bus from Deià to Orient.
I ask Don Antoni what the taxi service is like. He tells me
it won't be easy on a Sunday, but then, God bless the
man, he asks one of his sons, Pere, who helps out at the
hostel at weekends, if he will take me. I offer to pay for
the petrol, and all is settled. I have a chauffeur who will
drive me, bring me back and wait for me in the local bar
to give me privacy. I explain to Don Antoni that I need
to return to the place where my husband's ashes were

spread. He understands and doesn't pry further. Maybe that is one of the advantages of being seventy.

At four p.m. Pere, dressed in the usual uniform of jeans and white T-shirt, is waiting for me outside the hostel in his father's car. He has the dark curly hair and eyes that slant from so much squinting at the sun of many Mallorcans. I carefully lay a few sprigs of purple and red bougainvillea on the back seat and get in beside him. He is quiet and respectful and just mentions how hot it is for November. Apart from a few pleasantries, we head eastwards in complete silence. I have no wish to talk, and he doesn't either. Half an hour later the car is climbing the hill that leads to the tiny village of Orient. Pere parks the car near the entrance to the village. We get out and he hands me the bougainvillea. I tell him I will join him later in the local bar. He wanders off humming nonchalantly and doesn't look back to see where I am going. Whatever this old woman is going to do with her bunch of bougainvillea in Orient is of no interest to him at all.

To the right of where the car is parked there is a vast green field bordered by tall evergreen bushes. I climb over a low fence and walk through the coarse grass, stumbling over half-buried stones. When I am near the far corner of the field, I stop by the dry-stone wall. There is no sign of the urn that we buried under the thick foliage, which now grows over the wall even more dense and prickly than sixteen years ago. I take a few steps forward and place the bougainvillea on the grass. I close my eyes, enjoying the warm sunlight on my face. The music of birdsong, indifferent to the joys and tragedies of human beings, continues as it always has done. Butterflies flutter around and lightly brush my shoulder. Nothing can perturb this beauty, not even death or suicide. I feel, yet again, the circular pull of the planet and am gathered up in it. Nothing is lineal. I have turned another circle and returned. The buzzing silence and peace fills every atom of my being and suddenly I am grateful. I no longer fear death. As she moves closer, I am beginning to see her beauty. I take a pen and notepad from my bag and sit on the grass. This is my last arrival to the Mediterranean Island that has witnessed fifty years of my life and soon, my death.

***

Orient

Monday 2 November

Querido Javier,

Today is *el día de los fieles difuntos.* You have been one of them, the deceased, for sixteen years now, so what better day for writing you a letter I should have written to you when I fled Mallorca all those years ago? I hope you are listening wherever you are. I am sitting in your field, your sacred ground, where the boys and I spread your ashes with our bare hands, numb with shock and grief. I hope you are moving on, away from this earthly plane, because I know you have been around for too long. I have felt your ghost brush by me and smelt your cigarette smoke even with the windows open.

You'd be getting on for seventy-four if you had lived. I don't want to entertain the thought of what would have become of you if you had, and even though your death was tragic, you are probably better off dead. You never wanted to live anyway. You always said you wished you had never been born. I am an old woman now and you would most likely not find me at all attractive. You wouldn't like my thin face and thighs or my bony backside. There would be no cause for jealousy, no need to say, 'Why were you looking at him?' as we walked down the road, you gripping my arm till it bruised. There is a freedom in being old, in being almost invisible. I can do what I like, go where I want, stare at who I want and it doesn't bother anyone too much, as long as I don't cause any trouble. I gave you my beauty and my youth, but I wouldn't go back to the years I spent with you. No. They were years of fear, of being a victim, of ridiculous stoicism and absurd contrition. I no longer make excuses for myself or for you. I can see all the cracks and flaws in both of us. But in spite of the stinging scars, I've always wanted to live. I've always thought that burdens would get lighter and that I would find peace in my old age. Just feeling the sun on my face and all the life buzzing around me in this field lifts my spirits. But you never gave yourself the chance to pick up the pieces of your life, examine them through the eyes of old age and think *This wasn't who I truly am.*

I have tried to understand you, the traditions you were steeped in from birth. Women were servers of male needs and egos. You were unable to take on the baggage I carried from my own independent upbringing, my university education, my ambitions, my previous relationships. You could not envisage me as an autonomous being with my own needs and dreams. Anyone could see we were not suited, two foolish kids of nineteen and twenty-two. How did you cast such a spell on me, that I still thought I loved my jailor twenty-five years on? Stockholm syndrome, I think it's called. I must be a textbook case. I felt guilty constantly for making you suffer, for not being the person you needed me to be, and I stupidly imagined I could eventually make things right. At the beginning I thought no one could love me as much as you did. Maybe I fell for you because of that intensity. I also wanted to be able to love and sacrifice myself for you; to give you back all you gave to me. The naivety and innocence of a nineteen-year-old who had no parameters were my downfall, and yours.

But as I said, I know part of you is still around. I saw your ghost one first of November in Sam's house, when I went to visit him to try and heal the rift between us after your death. Maybe you wanted to help. You were dressed in the clothes you wore in the coffin: a blue jacket and grey trousers, a necktie which barely covered the red weal from the rope. I did not want to see you, Javier. I shut that image out. You could not frighten me in death too. And I heard you calling me twice. What did you want to tell me? If you want my forgiveness, you have it, with no 'buts', no caveats. But I think you deserve an apology from me, too, for the way I suddenly disappeared – althhough it was the only way I could have left. You deserve an explanation, a conversation, a final closure so we can both move on. If you had been more stable, we could have had that conversation before I went, but I feared your reaction, and for my personal safety, to such an extent that I had to flee in the traumatic way I did. I know how much I wounded you, how my fleeing knocked down the last support you held onto before you let yourself drop into the abyss. Then I imagine you were left with truths about yourself that were so painful that only anger could help you live with them, and the sadness was so brutal that only your soul could cry. I suppose those feelings had sunk so deep that just your final loneliness could help you bring them to the surface and look at them, unveiled and bleak. Suicide was the only escape. This is what I am most sorry for: your desperate loneliness, no one to hold your hand, to encourage you to build a new future. But you knew there was no future, no work, no partner, no illusion. Reality dealt you a huge blow and you no longer had the strength or desire to invent new fiction, new role plays to uphold the scaffolding of yourself. You must have seen before you a flat landscape, steppes with not even a scraggy tree to hang your hopes on.

I ask for your forgiveness for not having left years before when there was still time to start anew. I didn't have the courage to bear your hounding, neither was I going to leave the children behind as you used to threaten me with when in the darkest moments, I told you I could bear no more. Was it some kind of karmic bondage that kept us together for thirty-four years, a deep emotional rope that suffocated us both? Even though you were having affairs whenever you could, you were never able to break the cord. Did you think I was your property in a kingdom you reigned over? We are only kings and queens of our own souls, not of others. Who would have thought that in the end I was stronger than you? That steel would emerge from the heart of my gentleness. Now I have a life, however short, and yours has been over for many years. I am sorry for that. I wanted you to make a different one for yourself. But it was too late. You had fallen to pieces inside a long time ago with your confused amorality. Women had to be moral then, but not you. A pristine heart doesn't need the straitjacket of your double-standard morality, nor does it torture those who reject it. Yours was a flawed love, tainted by male chauvinism and jealousy.

You wouldn't stand a chance with the feisty women of today, Javier. Feminism rules, or tries to rule, because a small percentage of women in Spain are being murdered by partners who can't accept the new freedoms. But most women under sixty would wipe the floor with you. Your theories, and your father's, have crumbled into dust. Your *chulería*, your cockiness, and macho attitude would be mocked. Your mother would have denounced your father for much less than breaking a chair over her head. She would no longer get up from the sofa to see what the time was on the kitchen clock when he was too lazy to look himself, nor allow him to thrust her children's faces into the plate of soup when they wouldn't eat it. She would no longer wear a bitter half-smile, knowing that her idea of life was over the day she got married and that only small triumphs of deceit could keep her afloat. Times were changing fast when you were alive, Javier. Now you wouldn't know where to place yourself. So you are better off where you are, where you always wanted to be. Although you have missed meeting your grandchildren, who do ask what happened to you. We haven't had the courage to tell them the truth yet.

I wonder sometimes if we had been born earlier or later, before or after *la transición*, or better still, in the same countries, would our relationship have worked out, would we have continued to feel the intense joy and happiness that we did those first few months? Maybe then we would not have been unwilling victims of each other. But here I am, still in your beloved Mallorca which is now my only home and where my ashes will also be scattered. It won't be long now. My bone marrow is giving up the struggle to keep my blood healthy. Then all this ridiculous suffering will be dissolved into the soil and wind, and our little tragedy will be remembered for a few years by our families and the friends that remain, then forgotten forever. But may it all be cleansed from the psyche of our sons and our descendants. May the story end with us two, never to be repeated.

Did you have a moment of clarity before you died? What did you see and think in that final moment? Did you feel the sun on your face, as I do now, and maybe have an instant of regret for what you were losing? Did you remember the day we met? Did you understand your life with the sharp vision death grants us before we fall into its embrace? Did you know what you truly loved, who you were under the layers of bullshit? That on the other side of your jealousy and paranoia, beyond the demons, there was pure love. Or were you just glad to be rid of this life, to release your burden finally?

Wherever you are, I wish you love and redemption. I hope you are not still wandering but travelling up to where there is only light and peace, where there is nothing to be forgiven; just a constant expansion of the love you always held in your heart, Javier.

Acknowledgements

My thanks to Nicky Taylor for her expertise and sensitivity in editing this book.

Thank you to Jon Bowra, Emma Ellis and Samantha Meade-Newman for taking the time to read the manuscript and for giving me invaluable insights and feedback.

I am also very grateful to Emma and Samantha for writing the blurbs.

My thanks to Katharina Kühne for her enthusiasm and ideas for the cover design.

Thank you to my family and to my extended family of good friends who have accompanied me and put up with me on this long journey. I love you all.

About the Author

Heather Smith was born in Brighton, England in 1950. She studied English and Philosophy at Manchester University for two years before, aged twenty, she made the move to Mallorca, Spain.

A degree in Spanish Philology from the University of the Balearic Islands (UIB) followed and, in 2017, she was awarded an MA in Creative Writing from Oxford Brookes University.

Since retiring from teaching A-level English at a Majorcan secondary school, she dedicates her time to translation projects, running a book club and her own writing which she does in both English and Spanish.

In 2018 she published a book of poems: *Poems of Joy and Melancholy* (Ars Poetica, Oviedo, Spain). She contributed to a book of stories about Oxford in Spanish: *Relatos de El Trueno Dorado* (Editorial Sapere Aude). Her novella *The Last Months of Violet Koski* (Book Reality, Leschenault, Australia) was released in 2024 and she is currently writing a collection of short stories.

Heather is a widow and has two sons and four grandchildren.

www.ingramcontent.com/pod-product-compliance
Lightning Source LLC
Chambersburg PA
CBHW032014180726

48283CB00008B/2670